God made little apples

God made little apples.

JOHN D. SHERIDAN

Farrar, Straus and Cudahy
New York

God made little apples

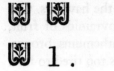

1.

The winter twilight was merging into deeper dusk as he stood on the pavement waiting to cross to the island at the base of the Nelson Pillar. But the light was not fading gradually. It changed at irregular intervals, like a spotlight at a pantomime. It was the old familiar trick of twilight in the city. When walls and buildings changed color you did not know whether the light was ebbing or swelling, and it might have been dawn instead of dusk.

When the traffic halted and the red scut lights went purring off towards O'Connell Bridge he crossed the street with the crowd. People bumped into him, or rounded him and passed him out, and he was the last to reach the footpath. He walked slowly and heavily in the narrow channel bordered on one side by black walls and iron railings and on the other by the orange boxes of the hawkers. Out of the corner of his eye he saw pyramids of fruit, and jugs of long-stemmed chrysanthemums, bronze, and white, and yellow. But he was too tired to look at them properly. He plodded on.

At the far side of the island he was blocked again by the mad stream of the traffic and he waited for the slim chit of a policewoman to raise an arm like Moses and give him safe passage. He looked down the canyon of Henry Street and saw it roofed with fire. Festoons of colored bulbs were stretched from side to side in great mosaics, and the half-tones of the twilight were lost in an iridescent sea.

It was still almost a month to Christmas, but that made no difference nowadays. The lights came before the shepherds. And he didn't like it. He didn't like it at all. He liked Christmas to be sharp and sudden, to take you by surprise and to come almost by stealth. That was how it had always come to the Glen when he was a boy. There would be no stir at all till Christmas Eve, and then, as soon as darkness fell, tall white candles blazed in every window and the whole Glen caught fire. It was as if squadrons of angels had carried tapers to the candles of Meentagh, and Carramullen, and Lurgabrack, and raced the dusk from valley to valley.

But now the lights of Christmas anticipated the feast. There were too many of them, and they came too soon. Advent was scarcely in, and Henry Street was a furnace glare. Shoals of colored lights played hide-and-seek among fixed stars of white and yellow, falling and climbing and wheeling in bewildering acrobatics. His eyes dazzled when he looked at them. He felt dizzy, and lost, and old.

He walked slowly and painfully under the sea of

4.

light, bullocking his way as if a heavy wind were pressing against him, and lifting his feet like a man travelling in a newly ploughed field. There was a lightness in his head and a sea-shell ringing in his ears.

His feet weighed him down. They had been good feet once, but the virtue had gone out of them. They had begun to die, and not before their time. Seventy years was a good spell, and it had taken a sore toll of his feet. They had to be lifted one by one, like the leaded boots of a sea-diver. They had been supple once, but there was no suppleness in them now. And the legs above them were tree-trunk thick, criss-crossed with knotted veins and red and blue pencillings, and scarred with dead ulcers.

He would go from the feet up, not like the old Dean above, who was mouldering in St. Patrick's, and who had gone at the head first like a stricken oak.

"That's a fine bit of an evening, Brother Bernard, thanks be to God."

It was one of the hawkers who had spoken to him: a great shapeless woman, wrapped in her shawl like a red Indian squaw and seated on a low stool beside a scaffolding of orange boxes and bread trays.

He stopped for a moment.

"Yes indeed, ma'am."

"Fresh and well you're looking, Brother."

He smiled and walked on. She had told a lie for his comforting, but he knew that when he was out of earshot she would wrap her shawl still tighter about her, rock a little on her stool, and follow him with her eyes like one expecting a sudden collapse.

"That's the old Brother from St. Michael's above. Brother John Alleluia. He looks bet, God help him."

He looked bet and he was bet. He was half sorry now that he hadn't taken a bus from the Pillar. It would have eased his feet. But when you were out questing and begging alms from door to door, you rationed your bus rides and didn't squander your pennies. The Bursar wouldn't mind, and the Prior had often told him not to overtax his strength by foolish economies and not to save on bus fares. But a begging friar was a begging friar. He could take a cup of tea if he was offered it; and a boiled egg was alms, not an indulgence. Besides, a friar less meant a ration more, and if you could feed yourself on the road so much the better. But Bernard never liked using the pennies he gathered. The hard cash was for the community.

He hated questing, and he was glad that he had to do it only once in a while, but he felt that it was good for him. It was like another noviceship, like a renewal of vows. When you worked in the kitchen and could get potatoes by putting your fist into a bag you were inclined to forget that you were a beggar by profession, that you hadn't a shilling to your name, and that you had opted of your own free will for the bag and the staff. Questing set your sights right again. It cut you down to size. You became a mendicant and knocked at doors: at all kinds of doors; at doors that remained shut, though the window curtains stirred; at doors that opened grudgingly, as if the chains were still on them; and at good decent Christian doors.

And you were never really welcome, not even at the Christian doors, for the first reaction to a begging Brother or a pair of begging Sisters was a frown. Sometimes the door slammed on the frown. Sometimes the frown changed to a smile, and you knew then that a good soul was suffering you for Christ's sake and offering it up. No one really liked to give, and it always hurt a little. That was why it was good to give; and good to ask.

He was past the hawkers' stands now, and he had a clearer view of the shop windows: marshmallow hats on silver-grey, eyeless heads, and golden girls with arms askew; sideboards and hot-water bottles and motoring helmets; sewing machines and teddy bears and more shoes than could ever be bought. The window he liked best was full of fowl and hams, cheeses like enormous red billiard balls, jars of transparent honey, carrots and cauliflowers, dates and apples. But what he liked better still was the bustle and press of humanity, and the noise and smell and color of the open market place—things that were as old as mule paths in the mountains.

He would come back to Henry Street and Moore Street a few days before Christmas, he told himself. The hawkers would be in full cry then: just now they were only warming up. They would be jammed stall to stall on the pavements and they would overflow into the gutter; exercising mechanical toys on bread trays, winding up sailors and mice and tanks and spotted clowns, crying holly and mistletoe and cotton-wool snow and synthetic frost.

They would be begging people to buy "the last of the long decorations," as if every new customer had arrived in the very nick of time, and with the subtle insinuation that their dishonest neighbors were passing off short decorations as the real thing. And they would show "Get your dancing giraffe!"

7 .

as if forgetful souls, or ones not well versed in the conventions of Christmas, might overlook so necessary a component of the feast.

Usually they shouted on the wind and spoke to the whole world, but they had the trick of the busker too, and once in a while they would abandon the general approach and pick out one person from all the rest, spiking their victim with hand or eye, and saying, as if they could read minds and divine needs, "Were you looking for sprouts, sir?" or "Did you want nice carrots, lady?"

He liked the balloons: white and green and blue and cherry-red; round as moons, bolster-taut as great German sausages, or deformed into grinning totem poles; held captive with cords and straining for the sky—as if they longed to float upwards and bounce endlessly among the lights.

Yes, he would come back to Moore Street a little before Christmas, when Advent was burning to its climax. Just now the whole thing was premature, and the fun had come before the feast.

The crowds were part of Christmas. It was good to be bumped and shoved and importuned. It got you into proper heart. There had been crowds in Bethlehem too; crowds and noise and confusion; laden camels and striped awnings and dark-skinned men selling carpets and spices and sweet wine.

As he passed Jervis Street, a fresh wind came up from the river. It banished the illusion of warmth that the massed lights had brought to him. It was a cold wind. The breath of winter was in it.

It was a bitter wind. It blew past the lighted windows of the hospital, and past the little park where ancient men sat on sunny afternoons and where the tombstones of the old graveyard were ranged along the wall. It was a salutary wind. It chilled the spirit. First the lights and the crowds, the noise and money-changing; then sickness, and age, and forgotten graves.

When he turned into Capel Street he faced into the wind. Capel Street too was roofed with fire, and the glare of it vexed his eyes. This had once been the cobbled road that led northward past Mary's Abbey to Fingal and the Boyne Valley and on then to the Gap of the North, to Foyle and Swilly and the mountain lands where he was born.

His thoughts followed it to the northern sea. In the Glen there had been no blaze of Christmas lights, no elaborate provisioning. A chicken for the pot was feast enough, with maybe a piece of fat corded American bacon to go with it; and you put sprigs of berried holly behind the holy pictures and the calendar in the kitchen that came from Springfield, Massachusetts, or Hartford, Connecticut, and was a boast for a twelvemonth. On Christmas Eve you hung up your stocking on the mantelpiece beside the white china dog with the black snout and golden eyebrows, or on the soot-stained iron bar on which the clean socks were ranged on Saturday nights; and the most you could hope to find in it in the morning was an apple, and a pencil, and some love lozenges from Manus the Shop's.

For the few luxuries that it knew, the Glen depended on its colonies, and in the days before Christmas everyone watched for Jimmy the Post. Thrift would pay the rent and buy bluestone for spraying, but it was letters with foreign postmarks that brought a roughness of ready money once in a while, and every child in the place could speak of Boston, Mass., or Philadelphia, Pa., as glibly as he spoke of Tirladen or Inniscarrig. No one went hungry at Christmas, but such feasting as there was depended on dollars from America and pounds from Scotland. If things were good with the exiles, the Glen thrived accordingly, and a woman coming back from Derryleigh on Christmas Eve might have with her a big curranty cake, a dozen red apples, and a few cheap toys—a colored rubber ball in a wallpaper pattern, a tin whistle, and a tiny doll which, in the morning, would peep from the mouth of a stocking like the head of a jack-in-the-box.

With these, or with less, the children of the Glen were content. But in the essentials they were well served. The story of Bethlehem was very real to them. They knew their mangers and their stables. They were friends to the ox and the ass. They lived in the hill country and their fathers kept sheep on the mountain; and the carpenter's son sat on the same bench with them at school.

At Capel Street Bridge, he waited for the pointsman's signal. Great surges of cars and buses moved east and west with cohorts of cyclists on their fringes. The press of the traffic frightened him, and the noise of it bothered his ears. The big policeman, shiny as a seal in his cape, raised one hand and beckoned with a white baton. The cyclists swarmed towards the bridge, or away from it, and the north-south traffic moved on with a great clashing of gears.

The cyclists going up-river were poised as for the start of a race, and he had barely reached the pavement of the bridge when they were off. They nearly took his heels with them. The pavement seemed very high above the level of the roadway, and it was an effort to raise himself on to it. He was surprised at his weakness, and a little frightened. But his fright had an objective quality. He was outside himself, watching. He was looking at a frightened man.

He stood for a while, irresolute. Then he walked to the low balustrade of the bridge and set his arms on it. His breathing was fast and shallow, and he had need of rest.

A Guinness barge shot out from under the cavern of the bridge with a great riot of smoke. He was too tired to look down at it, but he knew the story by heart. As soon as the front of the boat was clear of the arch, a man in a blue gansey with red lettering on it would hook the lowered funnel upright again over the great volcano mouth and the vomit of smoke would be tailored and channelled. Then the boat would go chugging on, lying low in the water, with arrowing ripples under its nose and a smother of white at its stern.

An almost invisible seagull looped its way up from the dark river, veered sideways like a bat and without any perceptible wing beat, and hung motionless, like a bird in a picture. On each side of the river the lines of spires and chimneys converged towards Kingsbridge and the sunset that had been. The green dome of the Four Courts was dark against a sky that was shot with crimson and purple and banners of flame.

It was a familiar landscape. He could have plotted it in his sleep. But there was a strange quality in it that evening. It might have been a foreign city in which he had wakened from a drugged sleep. His eyes would not focus properly, and he told himself that they were still dazed by the lights of Henry Street. Waves of weakness swept over him, the noise of the traffic muted and swelled capriciously,

11 .

and there was a ringing in his ears as of a great turbulence of blood.

He leaned his weight more heavily on the parapet of the bridge, but the cold stone offered no support. It gave before him like a fistful of oatmeal. It was a cardboard bridge, and it had less weight and solidity than the body that clung to it.

Suddenly, a steel hand pierced the wall of his chest and tightened like a vice. The pain of it took the breath from him. It was not like the pain of his tortured feet or the pain in his blood-suffused legs. It was not a remote or marginal thing. It could not be reasoned with, or endured, or sublimated. It was a strangling, screaming pain, and he knew it at once for what it was. It could be identified and labelled as surely as a toothache. It was life or death.

There was no swaying of advantage this way or that, no gradation, no incident, no stages. The battle was decisive, and lightning-quick. It was over when you drew your first quiet breath, or when you choked convulsively on your last. There was no remand, no reprieve. You won or lost in one blinding instant.

This thought branched into a dozen thoughts that lasted no longer than his first gasp of pain, and yet lasted forever. They were like thoughts in a dream, that lasted a lifetime and passed in a flash. He was young and old. He was catching satiny speckled trout in the Big Burn, he was watching his mother turning the heel of a sock and biting at the wool, he was listening to Master Friel pedalling a tune on the wheezy harmonium in the school. He was serving the Prior's Mass, and shaping brown paper rocks for the Christmas Crib, and frying sausages for the community dinner. He was thinking of the rack, and men on beds of spikes, and of saints

12 .

being roasted on slow gridirons and praising God in defiant hymns. He was thinking too of the days and weeks and years when he had had no pain bigger than a grumble, no pain that an aspirin wouldn't quiet, of the days when he could breathe the sweet air, and take his meat, and say his beads in the monastery garden with nothing to come between him and his prayers but his own feeling of well-being. He had taken all these mercies for granted and without seeing them as mercies, instead of going on his knees and giving thanks for blessings as big as sun and moon and stars.

All this flurry of thought was geared to an agony that was outside time. There was no unit for the measuring of it. It was a thunderclap and it was eternity. It went as suddenly as it came. It did not abate or quieten. It was and it was not, and he knew that he had been in the grip of some tremendous force that might have crushed him like an eggshell.

Before this, he had turned blindly from the parapet of the bridge and taken a few shaken steps on straw legs that crumpled under him. One hand went out to ease his fall, but the other, like his legs, was made of straw; and yet not like his legs, for it made no effort at all.

Afterwards he remembered that he had said no prayers. He had said no prayers at all. He was not a saint on a gridiron. He was an animal, suffering and bewildered. The vice grip had squeezed all that was human out of him. It was only now that he could pray.

He had no pain now, and the absence of it soaked him with happiness. It was like cooling rain to his parched spirit. People gathered round him, but they were only vague shapes. They spoke to him and he made answers in his mind, but the mouth that should have turned the answers into sound was the mouth that he had known in nightmares. It was the mouth of a marionette, and the strings that should have worked it were not functioning properly. It was a Venetian blind with tangled cords. It was all to one side, like Gourock. It was a poor, pitiful thing.

They tried to lift him. They put hands under his armpits. But there was no answering tension in his limbs, and they let him lie.

Someone raised his back and supported it, and there was a babble of voices. They wanted to know what had happened to him, and if he was all right, and he smiled to himself at the futility of the questioning. He should have been frightened, but he was not frightened. He was not thinking of life or death. There was only one thought in his mind. He could breathe and rest, and nothing else mattered.

A big policeman knelt down beside him. He could see his cap and the shine on the little chain on the collar of his overcoat.

Presently he was lifted up and slid into an ambulance like a tray into an oven. There was something black lying on his chest, and after some thinking he remembered that it was his hat. They did this at a field marshal's funeral, or at a cardinal's, he couldn't remember which. When they boxed the man up, they put the badge of rank on his coffin. They could put an apron and a potato peeling knife on his. He was a scullion and he worked in God's kitchen.

2 .

They slid him out as they
had slid him in. He was being delivered like a piece
of merchandise. He got the familiar smell of a hospital: warm, damp, pungent. There was no mistak-
ing it.

His sight was blurred, and consciousness came
and went. He knew that he would have to be identified and docketed. A white nun without a face
fluttered about him and he tried to help her. He
made unintelligible sounds with his mouth, and he
pointed to his overcoat pocket with the hand that
could still point. The little black book would give
her the clues she wanted, and a telephone call to
St. Michael's would do the rest: the little black
book with the names of streets and people, the
record of the offerings of the faithful, and Colman's cryptic signs. In his other pockets they would

15 .

find the two pounds twelve and odd that had taken him the best part of a day to collect, his stock of leaflets, his handkerchief, his beads, and the fountain pen that blotted his fingers. Damn the much else.

They took off his coat and waistcoat, collar and stock, and fastened a pyjama jacket about him. Afterwards he couldn't remember his boots coming off, but he remembered the speed and unconcern with which they slipped off his black trousers and substituted striped pyjamas. There was a focus of heat at both sides and another at his feet.

They gave him something in a glass, and he felt the quick jab of a needle. It wouldn't have bothered him had it been a pitchfork.

They would have rung St. Michael's by now. Brother Joseph would go flip-flopping along the corridor to bring the news to the Prior, and the Prior would look up from the book he had been writing for years, and would never finish, and say "This is terrible. Poor Bernard! We must see Kilian."

The Prior's book was the joke of the community. It was to be a history of old Dublin, and he was milking everyone: the Augustinians in John's Lane, the Franciscans in Merchant's Quay and Killiney, and the staff of the National Library.

Bernard liked the Prior. He was a good priest, and a kindly soul, and his father in God. But he was lost in dreams, and he flustered easily. He was not geared for emergencies.

Father Kilian, the Sub-Prior, was his prop and comfort. When things went wrong he always said "We must see Kilian." Kilian the stout, shrewd Kerryman, Kilian who never flustered, who knew what to do and did it. Kilian would be sorry, but he would take the news in his stride. He would make adjustments in the duty roster, say a few words in the kitchen, and the life of the community would go on.

All this fuss and worry would have been avoided, Bernard was thinking, if he had had the good fortune to collapse anywhere in the huddle of streets between the river and Guinness's and the Coombe. Had he fallen there he would have been recognised at once and sent back to the monastery in a cab or a milk lorry and settled quietly in his own bed. For that was his own territory. There he was Brother John Alleluia and as well known as a begging ass.

A begging ass he was, but he was only a substitute. Colman was the official quester. Colman had been at it for years, doing his rounds day in and day out as assiduously as an election canvasser; getting a shilling here, and a half-crown there, and nothing over the road, and marking everything down in his little black book. It was only when Colman was on holiday, or laid up with his great, rough, wharrumping cough, that Bernard went between the shafts and tramped the city. In these recent years the Prior had suggested to him more than once that questing was too much for him and that he should leave it to one of the younger Brothers; and often he had been minded to. But questing was good for him. Besides, stopping it would have meant giving in to age and weariness. It would have meant dying a little. Once you got out of harness you started to shrink.

There was another reason too. Questing freed him from his apron. It gave him the run of the city and enabled him to feel its pulsations. Ballybough and Killester, Donnybrook and Clonskea, Whitehall

17 .

and Glasnevin—they were all part of him. He had grown up in the Swilly country but he was a Dubliner by adoption.

But Colman was the better quester by far. Colman knew his trade. He was brisk and businesslike. He watched the clock, kept to a schedule, and rationed his chats. He had talk for everyone, but not too much of it for anyone. When he had got a contribution, and marked it down, and given his holy picture, and said his piece, he moved on; not immediately, like a Banbridge beggar, but with little delay.

Colman had a system. He marked more than shillings and pence in his black book. He scribbled "rheum" or "b in B" after the names of the faithful, so that, calling a year later, he could ask a woman about her rheumatism, or her brother in Cootehill, or the boy in the bank, and pass as a friend of the family.

Bernard knew his own faults as a quester. He wasted time without meaning to waste it. He liked looking at flowers in gardens, and babies in prams, and galleon clouds, and lorry-drivers changing gear, and seagulls wheeling over refuse dumps, and old men sitting on seats. He liked to stand and stare, and this was bad for business. If his knock was answered by a Donegal accent he would stay an hour and his takings would fall accordingly. Colman was different. Colman covered the ground and delivered the goods.

Bernard's place was in the kitchen, not on the roads. He liked paring apples and potatoes, and dicing up raw beef, and he was a good hand with rice pudding. But he got tired at times of pots and pans and smells, and then he would find himself thinking of fresh winds and green lawns and the foreshore at

18 .

Sandymount, and he might even fall to wishing that Colman would get a touch of lumbago; and then, to balance things up, he would pray that God would send Colman health and look kindly on his weak chest.

He also prayed for Brother Paul, and sometimes with his nails sharp against his palms. Paul was his assistant in the kitchen. He was a little barrel of a lad with a face like a Hummel statuette. Paul was young, and he would never be older; older or wiser. He was slow, dreamy, happy, and maddeningly forgetful. He attracted cats and beggars and stray dogs. He had some of the attributes of Saint Francis, and everybody loved him; but Bernard often had to offer him up, like neuralgia. Paul dawdled over his dishwashing, and put too much salt in the porridge, and let the potatoes boil to mush. He was slow and willing, awkward and happy.

Once he failed to find a worm in the lettuce, and it rose up later, like a charmed snake, from the Prior's plate in the refectory. The Prior, that quiet man, said nothing, but Kilian, of course, couldn't let it pass. He came to the kitchen afterwards and said, "You know, Paul, that abstinence on Fridays is enjoined by one of the commandments of Mother Church."

It was morning, and Sister Magdalena was looking down at him. She was small and plump and red-cheeked, and there was a light in her eyes.

"You had a good night."

"Fair enough, thanks." There was a dead feeling on one side of his jaw, as if he had had a tooth out, and he knew that his speech was slovenly.

"Now we must freshen you up."

She slid out through a gap in the screens and

came back presently with a basin and towel. She sponged and dried his hands and face. He was thinking that no one could dry a face properly but the man that owned it.

"What would you like for your breakfast?"

She brought him porridge and tea and scrambled eggs on toast, and she helped him unobtrusively in his eating, supplying for his dead left hand.

"Now you'll feel better," she said when he had finished. "I'll take this tray out of your way and you can have a nice sleep."

He did not feel like sleeping, but he must have dozed off, and when he opened his eyes again the Prior and Kilian were standing by the bed. They might have been ghosts, but they were solid and three-dimensional. But their living presence was no more real than his memories of them. He could bring them up in his mind at any time like prints in a developing dish: the Prior, tall, frail, sparse of hair, and with the mildest of grey eyes behind his spectacles; Kilian, squat, heavy-shouldered, powerful, and with microscopic hairs on his fleshy nose.

He sensed the strength of the bond that linked the whole community. They were closer than children of the same parents. They differed from one another like chalk from cheese, but they belonged to the same family. They quarrelled, and sulked, and got on each other's nerves, but they were all members of the brotherhood and they rallied like clansmen. You could count on every man Jack of them, on all who wore the uniform, wherever they were on God's green earth, or who had worn it once and were now moldering bones.

"How are you feeling, Bernard?" The Prior's voice was as mild as his eyes, and he never raised it.

Bernard said that he was feeling grand, but his

voice belied him, and the sound did not fully carry the sense. He could still feel the drag on one side of his mouth.

"That's good," said the Prior. Bernard could read their thoughts. They were assessing him, and trying not to show their concern. "You must take things easy for a while."

This was Kilian, the practical man, Kilian with his Kerry vowels and Kerry shrewdness. Kilian never fumbled his passes. If there was dry rot in the rafters, or a bread strike, or a rebuke from the Provincial, Kilian knew how to deal with it. A crisis was meat and drink to him. "Yes, you must take things easy."

Bernard raised the hand that still obeyed him and let it speak for him. What can I do but take things easy? I can't sign on for Shamrock Rovers, or jump a five-barred gate, or bring you the water and towel at the Lavabo. I'm tethered like a calf in a stack-garden. I'm spancelled like a dunting cow.

"There's nothing you want?" said the Prior.

"Nothing." It would have eased the poor man if he had asked for artichokes or the catalogue of the National Gallery.

"And you're feeling all right?"

"Grand, thanks, Father. Grand." That was the truth. He *was* feeling grand. There was pain in him somewhere, but it was drugged and tamed and quietened. It was only a shadow of the pain that he had known on the bridge. He was feeling grand.

Sister Magdalena was back again. "There's not a bother on him," she said.

She looked as pleased as a cat at milking time, but Bernard could read her eyes. The interview must finish. They were tiring the patient. Their time was up.

Kilian read the message too, but he was too shrewd to react at once. Nothing must alarm the man in the bed.

"We'll have him back again in no time," he said. "In no time at all."

"Yes indeed," said the Prior.

Bernard knew what they were thinking. They were thinking that the tide of life was low in him and that the hurt he had taken had numbed his mind as well as his body. They were frightened and were trying to hide their fright.

In a way, his mind had numbed a little. He had spells of drowsiness, and the things about him had lost their hard edges. They fused and coalesced. But that was the needle and the drugs. The things that killed pain closed down some links in the communication system. They slowed connections and made the operator nod at the switchboard. But what they cut off was the immediate and present. They did not deaden the mind nor banish its fancies. It did not bother about tomorrow's dinner but it could fill in with dreams and memories.

His visitors were gone now, and he had no clear recollection of their going. They might have been with him a minute or an hour.

He would have prayers now; a whole torrent of prayers. His name would go out in bulletins, and the brethren would supply for his weakness. In the meantime he could take his rest and get on with his thinking.

He thought first about the markets, and this was almost a matter of conscience. Strictly, he should have never gone near the markets at all. Victuals could be ordered by telephone, canvassers called to the door, and the monastery could get its fruit and fish and vegetables nearer home. But Bernard told himself, and the Prior at intervals, that by going to the markets occasionally he could save the community money. Colman went out questing every day, and a community which accepted charity was bound in justice not to squander it. Holy poverty meant watching ha'pence, and frugal living entailed thrifty buying.

The Prior never refused permission, but he always hesitated long enough to let Bernard know that it should not be asked too often, and to remind him that the place of a religious was in the pulpit, or the library, or the kitchen, according as God willed and his superiors directed. Whenever the Prior was away, Bernard had to ask Kilian for permission. Kilian never hesitated at all, but Bernard hated asking him. Kilian had a way of looking at you. He read your mind and made you feel small and imperfect.

In both cases, the frequency of the asking had some relation to the incidence and magnitude of Paul's blunders, and to Bernard's patience with them. When Paul was fair to middling, or when Bernard was strong in virtue, the markets were far away; they came nearer when Paul was having one of his bad days and Bernard was digging his nails into his palms.

He seldom reprimanded his cherub-faced assistant. He took a walk in the garden, or sliced carrots viciously, or counted up to twenty. When all else failed, he took off his apron and went to the markets. He went to the markets as another man might go to the public house.

Sometimes it was not Paul who tempted him. Sometimes it was the Flapper Flanagan. When things were bad with the Flapper, he would come

23 .

to the back door of the monastery for a bite to eat, and he always had news of the markets. If there was likely to be a glut of fish in the morning the Flapper would know about it, and if a lorry-load of Kentish plums had arrived too late for Friday's market Bernard would hear of it before night, and the community would buy an enormous cod for a few shillings or have stewed plums five days running.

Bernard did well in the markets, for he was a countryman and he had the dealing sense. And his black clothes and round collar were often a help to him. Cabbage was counted to him with easy arithmetic, and when he was buying swede turnips a few big ones would be thrown in as a tilly. Sometimes he might have to hire a jennet-drawn float to bring home his purchases, but usually they were delivered free by lorries going to Rialto or Terenure or the Coombe.

He liked the fruit market best. In the fish market, the bustle lasted only an hour or two, and you had to go very early if you wanted to look at its black snouts and gaping mouths, its freckled salmon trout and striped mackerel and blubbery ray. By the time Bernard arrived, the day's business was almost over, and the cement stretches looked cold and empty and forlorn.

The fruit market too had its mad hours, but its tumult never died completely. The auctions went on till eleven, and the tangle of carts and lorries did not thin down properly until nearly midday. He liked the fruit market, the smell of ripeness and rottenness, the shouts and the clamor, the sound of engines and hooves, the banter of the red-faced auctioneers on their rostrums. He liked hearing the shawled hawkers speaking of "pinanas" and "bidaydas" and "dimatas," and the way they simulated surprise when they were told the price of a case of oranges. He liked watching the stained country carts moving one by one under the auctioneer's hammer, their pyramids of Savoy cabbage arranged in cunning mosaics and with the smoothest, biggest heads on the outside. He liked looking at the polished skins of Spanish onions, clean and without blemish; the moon faces of melons and the bronze-gold of tufted pineapples; big Bramley cookers from Kilkenny, and perfumed eaters from the valleys of the Suir and Blackwater.

This seasonal wealth and profusion, this unending harvest festival, made him think often of the poverty of the cold northern valley where he had grown up. In the Glen, people sowed spuds and corn and turnips, and were hard set to find space for them. The only vegetables in the Glen, except for the carrots, scallions, and parsnips in the Master's garden, were the spindly spring onions sown to flavor the dinners of 'champ' and the big purple kale that was feeding for man and beast. Life was hard in the Glen, and there were no trimmings.

At Hegarty's, down by the shore, there were six or eight ancient apple trees. They were never tended or pruned, and the apples they bore were small, sour, and scabby. Apart from this, the only fruit that grew in the Glen came from the two plum trees and the solitary cherry that grew at Greens of the Milltown, where the road from Derryleigh turned left and then right before it dwindled into a stony lane and stopped forever on the edge of the tide like a road that had lost its way.

Hegarty's orchard was a wild, overgrown garden sheltered by rowan trees and whitethorn bushes from the headland beneath it. Old Tim Hegarty—he was as gnarled and crippled as his apple trees, and three times their age—lived alone in a miserable thatched cottage that had sunk with the years until its gable was no higher than the tangled fuchsia bushes that hid it from the road. He had three poor fields that the sea winds had taken the heart out of, and he labored them as best he could. He had a poor way on him. He boiled his few spuds, and washed his shirts, and climbed to the mountain on poor done legs to save his turf. He had no time for playing nursemaid to apple trees, and the little skill that he once had in the management of them had dwindled with his strength and his hopes. He was a bird alone. All the breed of him were dead or were in America, and he was ripe for the grave.

His trees were heavy croppers, but the apples were little better than crabs. Small as they were, he guarded them with miserly greed, and he stayed awake at night to balk the Glen boys when they came raiding, but he could not be always on the watch, and at least half his crop was carried off in the dark nights after harvest. The rest was sold in pennyworths. He would let you go into the orchard and fill your cap for a penny, and unknownst to him you could fill your pockets too.

Now and again, Manus the Shop would buy a barrel of American apples in Derry. It would be sent out by rail from the city and shipped across the Lough to Derryleigh, and one of the Glen carts would collect it at the pier. The opening of it would be a ceremony. Manus would tap up the wooden hoops, and prize up one of the lid panels with the point of his adze, and half the village would be there to see him do it. The apples had come all the way from Oregon or Nova Scotia, but they were still red, luscious, and unblemished. The sun was in them, and the good earth, and the smell of them went up the street. An American apple was a rare luxury, and when a Glen woman brought two or three of them home with her from the shop she would cut them carefully into quarters so that the whole family could share in the feast.

Bernard lay in bed and thought about the markets and about the people who worked there: Jer Kerrigan, and Raffler McGurk, Joeboy Mulligan and the Flapper Flanagan, Sam Garnley and Big Dennis and Katie Smith—Katie who had a stall in Moore Street and a fur coat and a ne'er-do-well husband and a heart of gold. They were God's people, the people you prayed for and preached at. They were "My dear brethren." They were real, and solid, and lovable, and if you tested them for charity you would get the full of your sieve.

He thought of "the Rush men," who lived in a sea-warmed peninsula sixteen miles to the north of the city and who came to the market on Tuesdays with carrots, leeks, sprouts, parsley, beetroot, and early potatoes. They loaded their carts the night before and set off in the early hours leading their horses. They would drink strong tea in the market restaurant or in one of the eating houses in the streets round about, and wait then till the morning rush was over and the salesmen had time to fill in their dockets and pay them off.

They were powerful men with enormous hands, and their thick necks were stained with the wind and the sun. They were men of the fields, and they stood out from the city-born porters and donkeymen, who were taller but had less bulk. The market workers could swing a barrel of apples or a bag of potatoes over the tail-board of a cart, because they had the trick of it, but the Rush men had brute strength to spare, and one of them would think nothing of taking two half-hundredweight weights in each hand and raising them above his head.

There was Norse blood in Fingal, and the Rush men were broad-thewed like their Viking forbears. They reminded Bernard of his own folk, though they bred bigger men in the Swilly country.

But he was thinking of the past, he reminded himself. Rush had moved with the times. Its men stayed at home now and sent their stuff to the market by motor lorry. He missed them sorely, for he had been reared on a farm and he spoke their language, and they had been a link with days that were gone forever.

It was his third morning in the hospital. The place was very quiet. There were three other beds in the ward, he knew now. He heard coughing and whispering and movements at times, but he did not know his roommates. There were screens round his bed. He was segregated and apart. Sister Magdalena slid through the arras at intervals, like a character in a play. Sometimes she brought him medicine or drinks or food, but most times she just looked at him and smiled, or made a pretense of smoothing his pillow. She took his pulse and his temperature. She was watching him like a hawk, and he knew that he was not out of the wood yet.

He was surprised by the intensity of his thinking. Impressions flooded his mind, and old, old memories. They were old, but they were real, and vivid, and detailed. He could feel the coldness of the Big Burn poulticing his ankles as he crossed the stepping stones below Doherty's meadow, and the wetness of a panting trout in the grip of his fist. He got the smell of peat smoke, and the homespun smell of the church at Sunday Mass, and the faint smell of potato blossoms. He saw his mother raising the black, three-legged pot a notch or two when the porridge was snoring nicely, so that it would be in no danger of burning and would have a skin on it at supper time. They took their *brohan* thick in the Glen, and when it was cold you could spoon it out in slabs.

He saw the smoke-blackened map of Europe on the school wall, and he heard the soft padding of bare feet as the scholars toed the circle marked by round-headed nails on the schoolroom floor and waited for Master Friel to hear their lessons. He knew parts of some of the old lessons still. He could hear the Infants singing out "Tom is on the moor with his dog and gun," and one of the big girls reading "Warren Hastings attributed the small-ness of his stature to the hard and scanty fare of the seminary in which he had been educated."

At playtime, the scholars ate their pieces of but-tered scone (they were thick slices and well larded with butter) in the little schoolyard that was shadowed by the bulk of the mountain. It served as a schoolyard, but it was merely the irregular space bounded by the school porch and the wall of the chapel yard and the Master's byre. It was a right-of-way for the Meentagh folk coming to the shop, and for the Master's cows; and the old age pensioners crossed it on Fridays, for Master Friel ran the Post Office as well as the school and ca-tered for both old and young.

On hot summer days, forms were sometimes car-ried out of the school and classes would be held in the open, and the Master's hens would pick their way under the bare legs of the scholars, or peck at the wooden floor of the porch and have to be shooshed out. The air would be filled with the hum

29 .

of insects, and when a cart rattled down the road to the shore the driver would touch his cap and shout "That's a bully day, Master."

The smell of the school was still in his nostrils. It was the smell of ink and paper, of homespuns and ancient desks. He could see the round, slow-ticking clock, and the Master's rostrum, and the press where the chalks and pencils were kept, and the low harmonium with its crimson cloth peeping through the lattice work like the Canon's stock. He fingered the geranium leaves, so firm and furry to the touch, in the pots on the windows. The windows were small and deep-silled. On one side they looked out on the chapel yard, and on the other on the green and purple of the mountain, on black peat scars and granite outcroppings.

He was back to his beginnings, and he wondered, without panic or forebodings, if the prelude to death was a review of life, the sort of stage-by-stage conditioning that eases deep-sea divers up from the depths. Was there a transition that helped to bridge the gap between the sequence and trial and error that was time and the eternal present where knowledge was a white unmeasured flash, where there was no learning or unlearning, no fumbling or uncertainty?

But he was not dying. He knew that. He might be in danger of death, but he was not in immediate danger. If he were dying there would be a stoled priest, and candles, and holy oils, and the prayers that summoned the saints and banished Satan. If he were dying he would be shriven, and the white Host would be laid on his lips, and he would be escorted to the threshold. The nuns would see to that. They ministered to the body; they bandaged it

30 .

and healed it and timed its functions on charts; but their real concern was the soul. They wanted to keep the breath in you as long as possible, but they watched for its flickering and they did not let you go until you were vouched for and accredited.

He was not dying, but he might easily have died. He might have died clinging to the parapet of the bridge. And then there would have been no conditioning, no time for adjustments. He wondered what happened to the soul when the flame of life was quenched as suddenly as the flame of a candle after benediction. Was the shock of passing eased for it? But perhaps there was no need for any such easing. Perhaps the soul, once it was free of the body, burgeoned immediately in its own proper element.

He had not died on the bridge, and he was glad of the respite. It would have been a cold, lonely way to go. He would have a week, or a fortnight, or maybe longer. He might even see his apple trees again.

There were four apple trees in the monastery garden: two Bramley cooker, and two Charles Ross —big succulent eaters that did not last over Christmas. They were big trees now, but they had been small once. They had come from Kilkenny wrapped in sacking and with earth about their roots. They were good pedigree strains grafted on quince stocks. Grafting was one of God's mysteries. You stuck a slip into a crab stock, and it was no longer a crab. You changed its nature. You waved your magic wand and your crab became a Cox's Orange Pippin, or a Charles Ross, or a Worcester Permain. And now they were doing still more wonderful things. They could put three grafts on the same stock and have three apple trees in one.

He had planted his four trees, scarcely daring to hope that anything so slender and fragile could survive the first winter. But they did survive. They grew big and strong and vigorous, and the thrushes whistled in them. They put out buds, and leaves, and new branches, and they fruited when they were ready.

Bernard became an authority on apple trees, and old Andy Finnegan was his tutor. Andy had been a gardener with a retired admiral out at Ballybrack, and when he himself retired he came to live in the shadow of St. Michael's. He taught Bernard how to spray and grease-band, and that proper pruning would eliminate crossing branches and give a tree an open heart and prevent it from making too much wood. And he helped him cure the biggest Charles Ross of an attack of canker.

It was growing in a wide circle of soil, Andy said, and getting too much nitrogen. The thing to do was to sow grass in the circle. The community derided Andy's diagnosis and laughed at Bernard's faith in it. But Bernard sowed his grass seed, and in due course the canker healed. It left angry scars, admittedly, and one whole branch withered and died, but the tree still fruited and bore heavy crops, and Andy was vindicated.

Bernard gathered his apples lovingly, stored them where the air could get at them, and turned them at intervals lest the weaklings should corrupt their neighbors. By Glen standards he had an immensity of fruit, but there was no shortage of mouths to eat it. The community stretched to thirty or more when all the missioners were resting and none were afield—and the fruit from four apple trees made no appreciable difference in the housekeeping accounts or in the diet of the brethren.

But having its own apple trees made the monastery more monastic and linked it with primitive foundations where the brethren had sowed and reaped and gathered, where there were cows in the byre, and straw beehives in the garden, and handlooms under the sloping roof. Bernard was proud of his apple trees. They brought St. Michael's into line with tradition. He loved them for themselves, and because they answered some call in the blood. He had been reared to plough and spade, to seed time and harvest and the patience of the fields.

The soil in the monastery garden was black and sooty. It had been part of the city ever since the Vikings came to it, and centuries of smoke had put a skin on it. Until Bernard came it had grown nothing but grass, and that was the way the Prior (his first Prior, old Father Angelus, God be good to him) had wanted it. He had not forbidden Bernard's gardening, but he had never encouraged it. "Plant a few things if you like, Bernard," he had said, "but leave us our grass. We want a place where we can walk and breathe the good air, not a vegetable garden."

So Bernard had to be content with a few pocket-handkerchief plots near the wall and token plantings of lettuce and sweet pea. But when Angelus went to greener pastures, Bernard was given a free hand. He left the community its walks and grassy squares, but he grew cabbage and scallions and shallots, a few roses, and clumps of chrysanthemums that waited on the first frosts. There was never any profusion, for he lacked both the space and the time to achieve profusion, but he had a garden in which there was change and sequence and where the seasons could write their story.

Best of all, he had four apple trees: four tenacious apple trees that thrived like street urchins and took no hurt from the soot. In winter, they were like rheumatic old men with twisted limbs. There was no grace in them then, no comeliness, no promise. But the sap rose in them with the lengthening days, and soon after Easter they were a flurry of blossom. For a week or so then they wore white and were as young as the year. By day, the white was faintly flushed with pink, but the pink ebbed when the shadows came, and then they were white as snow. They seemed to give out light then, as if they had the quality of incandescence, as if they stored up light during the day and gave it out in the gloaming, as flagstones give out heat when the sun goes down.

The blossoms went, and then the little apples came. But the strange thing was that you never noticed them until they were as big as marbles. You came out one morning and rubbed your eyes. It was as if the little apples had grown miraculously during the night.

The Glen folk had a saying for it. "As sure as God made little apples," they said. All praise was in that, all thanksgiving. God made little apples, and no one else could have made them. God made little apples, and each was a separate creation.

Bernard lived with theologians and philosophers, and while some of them approved of his gardening, some of them felt, as Father Angelus had felt, that the monastery garden was too small for tiny dribbles of lettuce and old maid flower beds, and that green grass was enough. But Bernard cultivated his garden, and nursed his apple trees, and made his own theology, beginning with the tiny burnished seed that contained within itself the shape and height and girth and glossiness of the tree that was to be, and never reached the end of his thinking.

He made his own theology, checking at times with Father Austin, who was one of the luminaries of the Order. Laws were laws, but they were not directives that stars and seeds obeyed blindly, but rather the observed pattern of divine order. The universe was not a clockwork toy wound up and left to fend for itself, with each part carrying out its functions unerringly and of itself. God was everywhere and always in His world. He rounded every seed and shaped every snowflake. The rising of the sun was not a trick taught once and for all, but a daily assignment and summoning.

When Father Austin spoke about it, it was like a mighty poem. Without God's help, and knowledge, and presence, no one could sneeze, or score a goal, or raise a glass, or scratch his poll. Without Him, nothing rose, or fell, or barked, or wagged, or burned. He stirred the fronds in ocean caves; and the continuing existence of every swordfish, the charted orbit of every planet, depended on His remembrance and consent. He watched over fleas and men, and valves and pistons were as much His business as blossoms and cyclones. His hand held every rudder, His thumb print was on every chart. Wherever there was life, or movement, or matter, or spirit, He was. The universe was a diverse and complex business, but every part of it was under direct and personal supervision.

Bernard thought of his apples until he was tired

and sleepy. He thought of the earth as a bigger apple, capped with ice at the poles, spinning ceaselessly and carrying with it its prisoned, living waters, darkness and light, wind and calm, tropic and tundra: a tiny nutmeg in the immensity of space. And everywhere, always, God was. He timed the plunge of the walrus and plotted the fault cracks in icebergs. The thunder was His, and the hurricane; all stresses of bulk and force; all movement and equipoise, all growth and decay. He breathed into everything that breathed and moved everything that moved—not just as the first cause but as the continuing and necessary cause of being and reality. All that existed outside Himself he had called into being and kept in being.

Bernard had got the bones of it from Austin, but he had filled in the details himself and made of it a satisfying meditation. Now, with a Rosary for tailpiece, it filled in for his night prayers, and he dozed off somewhere in the last decade.

He was a week in the hospital now—a week all but a day. The screens were still around his bed, but the other patients spoke a little more loudly now. They were only voices to him, but he was beginning to know their voices. He was making some progress. The drag on his mouth had eased a little, and there was a touch of life in his dead arm.

The nights were the worst. Once the noises of the traffic thinned down, it was a long long time till the first milk carts. He knew that he slept a little, but there were mornings when he could have sworn that he hadn't closed an eye.

But the mornings always made amends. They

were the best part of the day, and when the light strengthened he felt his heart lift.

There was Mass in the hospital chapel at seven o'clock, and the chaplain brought him Holy Communion after it. He could time the hospital Mass roughly from his missal. But before that he thought of Masses everywhere: Kilian's Mass and Austin's Mass, and the Prior's Mass; Masses in New Guinea and Tunis; an unending sequence of Masses that followed the sun, and all of them bespeaking a place of refreshment, light, and peace for all that rest in Christ.

He repeated his own mementos several times every morning, praying for the members of the Order who were scattered in graves the world over, for his own kith and kin in the crowded graveyard at Killard within sound of the Swilly waters, and for Sam Garnley. He liked to slip in Sam's name with those of his own father and mother, sisters and brothers, uncles and aunts and cousins, sept and tribe and clan. He liked to bracket him with the clean of heart, for Sam had never been noted for cleanness of heart. He was Henry the Eighth in a bowler hat and brown shoes.

Sam had left Dublin as a young man, after failing his second medical for the third time, and with his half-year's fees in his pocket. He spent two years in London, sleeping in doss houses and on the Embankment, shovelling snow, carrying sandwich boards, and foraging in restaurant dustbins. But on his father's death he came into his inheritance as an only son: two thousand in Bank of Ireland Stock, three thousand in Guinness's, and a long-established business in the fruit and vegetable market. Everything had fallen into his lap.

He was in the early fifties when Bernard knew him first: a big fleshy man with a bulge to his stomach, and "a face on him like a bowl of blood," as the Glen folk used to say of old Colonel Redford. Sam used to boast that he had left the Church and that he had no use for priests or praying. "You haven't left it," Bernard said to him once. "You're still in the porch. You won't come in and you're afraid to leave. You won't do one thing or the other. You're like a boy with a smut on him bumming and boasting to give yourself courage."

But that was years later, and when they had learned to know one another better.

It all began on a brisk November day when Bernard asked the price of Sam's potatoes.

"Eight shillings a sack." The man with the red face snapped the answer round the end of his cigar.

"Would you give me three sacks for a pound?"

"No, nor for twenty-three shillings."

"I'll give you a guinea."

Sam took his cigar from his mouth and shook his head. Bernard was not abashed. This was market technique, and he revelled in it. When you were reared in the Glen you had the dealing instinct. It was meat and drink to you. It was in your blood. It was the fun and drama of the fair.

Just then, two Little Sisters of the Poor came to Sam's bank and stood waiting. They were silent questers; patient, wordless, self-explanatory.

The younger of the two was tall and good-looking; the other was small and sharp-faced. They hunted in pairs.

Their van came to the markets once a week. It was a converted Black Maria that they had bought for a song from the Department of Justice. It was like an enormous hearse, but it suited them. The driver sat on deck, with a rug about his middle, and the nuns, sitting in the sentry-box annex at the back, remained enclosed religious.

The Little Sisters would take anything—turnips, scallions, oranges, fresh herrings, money, or abuse. But they asked for nothing. They just stood and smiled.

"Give the Sisters a few cabbage," Sam shouted to one of his workmen.

"God will reward you, Mr. Garnley." The older Sister was a little Frenchwoman, and after thirty years in Dublin she still spoke with a foreign accent. "God will reward you, and we will get the old people to pray for you. They pray every day for all our benefactors."

"A fat lot of good that will do them," said Sam.

But he didn't say it to the Little Sisters, who had moved away a little and opened their sacks. He said it to Bernard.

"The Sisters do some good in the world," he went on. "But you fellows do damn all, apart from craw-thumping."

"Musha, maybe we don't do very much. But the Little Sisters do a spot of praying too."

"Christian charity I'm talking about, not praying. When I was down and out in London the only people who did anything for me were the Salvation Army and the street-walkers. I might have starved for all the priests cared."

"Whatever you did," said Bernard, "you didn't starve. Or if you did, you made up for it since. God bless you, but you show the signs of your meat."

"I earn my keep, if that's what you mean, and that's a lot more than you can say for the priests. Why should they expect the people to put clothes on them and fill their bellies? I'd as soon support the Christy Minstrels."

"You'd get better singing from them anyway," said Bernard. "Did you ever hear Father Benignus singing a High Mass? The poor man hasn't a note. And he hasn't much of a stomach either. He's as thin as a lath. But then he was never fed by the Salvation Army."

Sam flicked the ash from his cigar. "You have the gift of the gab."

"If I have there's two of us in it. But tell me, how much will you take for three bags of potatoes, now that we understand one another?"

"Twenty-four bob."

"Twenty-two."

"Twenty-three."

"I'll give you twenty-two and sixpence."

"Oh, very well. Take the damn things. But it's pure daylight robbery."

"We'll make it up to you," said Bernard. "I'll get the community to pray for you."

"Oh, go to hell," said Sam.

Sam was dead now for more than twenty years. He had dropped one day like a felled ox. Sam was dead. His flesh had putrified into smells and gases, and crumbled into gray dust. Sam was dead, but he was not forgotten. The Little Sisters prayed for him, as they prayed for all their benefactors living and dead. Sam's apples and York cabbage and white turnips were earning dividends in perpetuity. The Little Sisters prayed, and their wheezy old men and snuff-taking old women prayed with them. The old men held their beads in tired, blue-veined hands, and garbled their decades, and the

40 .

old women were too sleepy at times to give much heed to what they were saying; and the soiled prayers of the old folk fused with the white prayers of the Little Sisters to make a composite, communal intention—that Sam's sins would be forgiven him, and that Christ's blood would wash him clean. They had eaten his onions and Kerr's pinks, and his half-sovereigns had bought them camphorated oil, and red flannel, and snuff, and black, pigtail tobacco, and all this charity was bulked with a torrent of prayers on the credit side of the complicated spiritual bookkeeping that recorded the wayward life of Sam Garnley.

Sam was dead, and so was the Flapper Flanagan, who had run his errands for twenty years; who had brought his shoes to the mend, and helped to unload his plums and tomatoes, and swept the bank, and hobbled out to the market gate to summon donkey boys and yoke men. The Flapper was barely forty when he died, but no one could have guessed his age. Both his legs were affected with some congenital palsy, and his feet flopped grotesquely when he walked. He had a puny body and an enormous head. The right side of his mouth drooped, and his speech was distorted and labored. He had a stunted mind and a stunted body, and all he asked was toleration.

But such toleration as came his way was given grudgingly. The market porters and donkey boys pelted him with rotten lemons, and pulled his cap down over his eyes, and stuffed nests of young mice down his back when they found them in banana crates, and laughed at his incoherent profanities. But there was no malice in his curses, no resentment in the oaths that he mouthed. It was

41 .

better to be tormented than to be ignored. It meant
that he was accepted, that he had links, that he was
one of a community.

The Flapper worked on Sam's bank, but no one
had hired him and officially he was not one of the
staff. He was neither porter nor salesman, clerk or
lorry driver. He just hung about, and counted
heads of cabbage during the busy hours, and tied
onions into hanks, and helped at loading and un-
loading.

He got fifteen shillings a week from Sam for
these uncommissioned tasks, and an occasional shilling from customers in between. With this he was
happy. He counted his infinitesimal blessings. He
wore Sam's old overcoat and Sam's old shirts, he
stuffed brown paper into Sam's discarded hand-
made shoes, and he went home every night to an
attic room on the quays where he had old sacks for
covering and rats for company.

Times were always bad with him, but when they
were worse than usual he would come down to the
monastery at night and Bernard would give him
bread and meat or a bowl of soup in the back hall.
He ate like an animal, ravenously and with little
grunting noises. And when he had finished and
wiped his mouth with his sleeve and given thanks
he would talk about the markets and Sam Garnley.

Talking was a penance to him, for his mind
worked slowly and his mouth struggled with the
words, but he always talked at the monastery—as a
sort of extra grace after meals, and because some
innate gentility in him made him realize that it was
bad manners to hurry off after receiving a charity,
and also because in the monastery he was with his
own. For the Flapper was a religious perforce.
His disabilities were his enclosure. He lived his

own interior life, and he wore the ancient habit of Lazarus. The world and its noises were like a dream to him, and the life that ebbed about him scarcely touched him.

He had no memories of kith or kin, and no one knew who had begotten or reared him. He was one of the world's strays. But he had found his niche. He hung about Sam's bank like a fool at the court of the king, and he took Sam's scoldings and cursings with the patience of a stray cur, keeping out of the way for a while in the height of the storm, and then creeping back again and taking comfort in a conditional acceptance. If he had had a tail he would have wagged it.

His loyalty to Sam was absolute and complete. He said "Yes, Mr. Garnley" and "No, Mr. Garnley" and "Of course, Mr. Garnley." He always spoke of Sam as "the Boss," and he said it as if a genuflection should go with it.

When Sam died, the market had no place for the Flapper Flanagan. Sam's bank went to his nephew, and the Flapper was sent about his business. A rotten Christian had succored him, and now no good Christian thought him worth his keep. He left his attic room to the rats and slept in hallways. He begged outside the public houses that opened early to accommodate the cattle market, he gathered rags in the Corporation dumps and sold them for ha'-pence. And at night he came to the monastery as surely as the shadows.

Now he talked only about Sam. He remembered the golden age.

"God be with poor Mr. Garnley," he used to say. "He was a good man. I'm lost without him."

"You don't forget to pray for him?"

"I do not forget him, Brother. He was a good

man. I pray to God and His blessed Mother for him every night. Indeed I do. Why wouldn't I? He was always good to me. And sure who else have I to pray for?"

He had little need to pray for himself. He was one of the Lord's afflicted. All he had to do was to endure his time and wait. And he kept reminding God that Sam Garnley was a good man.

The Flapper died on a snowy night. His boots were full of holes and his lungs were full of rottenness. He was found lying in Mary's Lane, near the markets, making no more stain on the whiteness than if an old coat had fallen from the flapping racks outside one of the old clothes shops.

An ambulance brought him to Jervis Street, where they stripped the last of Sam Garnley's shirts from him, and wrapped him in a flannel nightshirt, and laid him in a clean bed. No one had ever fussed over him before, but he was fussed over now. They dosed him with miracle drugs, but he was too far gone for miracles, and the heat that was ebbing from him was beyond staunching. The chaplain leaned over him and heard a flea-bite Confession that must have made the angels laugh, and gave him food for the journey, and anointed him with holy oils. He prayed the saints to receive him and bade Satan begone. He could not have done more for Charlemagne.

Sam was dead, and the Flapper Flanagan was dead, but Bernard still lived. Sam had dropped in his tracks and never stirred again. "The heart it was," people said. "Took him sudden it did. But sure it must have been pickled in whiskey."

Bernard had a heart too, and it was still beating. It was a very important heart. Dr. Williamson, the specialist, listened to it occasionally, Dr. Kerrigan, the resident, heard its confession twice a day, and Sister Magdalena knew it better than she knew her own. It was a spoiled and pampered heart. Its doings were marked on wall charts and its tantrums eased by needles and drugging.

Whether he had a heart in the sense that Sam Garnley had had one was another question. He had made his own diagnosis, but so far no one had corroborated or opposed it. Not that it mattered very much. There were thousands of diseases, but only one of them was fatal.

The heart was a time bomb, and every beat it gave was subtracted from a fixed and pre-ordained total. To live was to die slowly, and death started the moment you were born.

He had seen death many a time. He had gone home from the novitiate to see his father die after long months of suffering had wasted the flesh from his limbs and brought out the bony architecture of his face. He had seen Father Sebastian die fighting for breath, and Brother Colum fall asleep like a child. But every death was sudden. Every death was an instantaneous change that stopped you in your tracks and gave reality to thoughts that had to be taken on trust on gusty days when the body exulted and the lungs sucked in the wine-sweet air. The thing that went could not be localized in ear or finger. It was not an organ or a function. It could not be seen, or measured, or touched, and it left behind it nothing but corruption.

Death was a thought that you went to sleep with, but you woke up to life, and every morning was a promise and a boast. And even in the hospital there was no blotting out the morning. It poured unhindered through the window's upper panes,

45 .

which were of clear glass, and sparkled in the lower panes, which were muffled and pearled. He had only a half view of the window, but it sufficed, and he could judge the intensity of the light by the whiteness of the ceiling and the sparkle in his bed-side tumbler.

It was a sunny morning and the tiny ward was full of light. Bernard was thinking of another sunny afternoon, and of Father John Chrysostom, who had taken his Master's degree in English Literature at Cambridge and had never forgotten it.

John Chrysostom was Rector of one of the Order's colleges in Australia. He was big and hand-some, and he had the head of a statesman. He had the head of a statesman and a voice to go with it —a rich, melodious, booming voice. John Chryso-stom leaned on his vowels and watched his elocu-tion. If he were asking you what kind of a day it would be, or where he would get a bus for Inchi-core, he could make it sound like a bit of Shake-speare. He was bland and smooth and sure of himself.

After he had spent ten years in Australia, John Chrysostom got a six months' holiday in Ireland, and he spent a month of it in St. Michael's; a great, booming month. He boomed when he said "Good morning" to the Prior, and he boomed when he asked Bernard how things were going in the kitchen. He had come from a sunny climate, and Ireland did her best to make him feel at home. John Chrysostom's month was a pet month. Ber-nard sweated in the kitchen, and John Chrysostom walked the streets wearing a light alpaca jacket and a straw hat. The brethren saw nothing wrong in the alpaca jacket, but they thought that the straw hat was not in the Irish monastic tradition, and they were glad that their visitor mitigated the tiny scandal by keeping to clerical black.

John Chrysostom set off for Australia again in due course, booming his farewells, but he left his jacket and straw hat behind him, and they became part of the community wardrobe. Bernard adopted the jacket and wore it occasionally in the garden and around the house. He wore the straw hat only once, and it was a long time before he could resurrect the memory of it without blushing.

It was a warm August day, just a year after John Chrysostom's departure. The sky over St. Michael's was as blue as any that Brisbane could boast of, and the sun was a tropic sun. It burned into walls and pavements. It made you think of creaking springboards, and white sails, and the lilt of the tide on seaweed-skirted rocks. Bernard wore John Chrysostom's alpaca jacket, but the sweat poured from him when he fuelled the black cooker and he had a sore time of it trying to keep the butter from running like water.

Some time in the afternoon the Prior asked him to collect a parcel from a shop on the quays. He was glad of the break. It would be good to get a breath of air and to be free of the kitchen for a little while. But he would be walking in his own heat and under his heavy black hat, and it was a fair step to the quays and back.

As it happened, he did not wear his heavy black hat. He wore John Chrysostom's straw. It was a sudden impulse, and, looking back on it afterwards, he could never explain it. He wore the black straw hat, and he would not have been much more conspicuous in a Turkish fez.

The straw hat was porous and feather-light,

and it shaded his eyes from the glare of the sun. But instead of feeling cool, he felt hot and bothered. People spoke to him and then looked after him. He had become a public spectacle. The thing had a nightmarish quality. It was like one of those shame dreams in which a man finds himself walking abroad without his trousers.

He brazened it out until he had passed the arch that links the two parts of Christchurch, but his courage had ebbed completely before he reached the quays. At the bottom of the hill he panicked and turned tail. The only thought in his mind was to get back to St. Michael's as soon as possible.

As he turned for home, two small boys came out of a doorway and looked at him. He could read their minds. He was a visiting priest, up from the country or newly arrived from foreign parts. He was fair game. They touched their forelocks reverently, and then they trotted by his side crying "God bless you, Father—give us a penny."

But Father gave them no pennies. Father shooshed them off. Father wanted to be left alone. But they followed him up the hill, circling like terriers, stepping backwards in front of him, and crying all the time "God bless you, Father. Give us a penny."

In the shade of the arch, he turned and faced them. "Run away! Run away! I'm not a priest, I tell you. I'm not a priest."

Silenced momentarily by what seemed a bigoted and sectarian rebuke, the boys drew back to consider the situation. They had been cruelly deceived and they had wasted their blessings. They had proclaimed the Faith profitlessly, and now the only thing to do was to deride the heretic. So they followed Bernard to the top of the hill shouting "Dick the minister!"

He had hoped to smuggle his misery into St. Michael's, but Brother Cyprian saw him coming in, and that was that. Cyprian pretended not to notice that anything was amiss, and simulated the custody of the eyes, but before long the whole monastery was humming with the news. Next day, Mike Delaney, one of the Confraternity prefects said to Bernard, "I seen those two chislers running after you yesterday, Brother. They want their backsides warmed." Bernard knew then that his shame was public property.

That evening, the Prior came into the kitchen making small talk—it was a fashion of his when he had something on his mind. He always put up a smoke screen before he attacked. Just before he left he said: "What's this I hear about you denying the Faith?"

Bernard chopped up carrots and talked to himself. He blamed the heat, and his own foolishness, which was fair enough, but he also blamed John Chrysostom, which was completely unfair. But he made it up to John Chrysostom: he included him for a while in his special intentions. He prayed that his voice would grow still more melodious, that his elocution would never falter, that his shadow would never grow less, and that Rome would add to his laurels by making him a Doctor of Sacred Scripture.

3.

Sister Magdalena came in to give him an injection. She pierced the rubber top of the phial, and raised the plunger carefully until a tiny bubble shivered on the point.

Bernard watched her without enthusiasm and turned on his side.

"This is your last," she said.

"Thank God for that."

He gritted his teeth before the needle went in, and he winced at the bite of it. The first injection had been nothing at all, but they had become sorer and sorer. Now every prod was like the sting of a wasp, and the pain swelled out in the taut muscles of his hip.

Magdalena gave him no sympathy at all. She pulled out the needle, dabbed at the puncture

50.

with cotton wool, drew up the bedclothes again, and said "There!"

He wondered how he would have reacted in the Colosseum. If he balked at this tiny stabbing, how would he have faced up to the bite of the slavering teeth? He thought of mild Father Sylvester, who had been tortured by the Communists in China, and who talked about it (when you could get him to talk about it) without rancor or heroics. Sylvester had told him that at times the pain would leave him completely and peace would flow over him like an anaesthetic. That, he said, was when his Christians were praying for him. It would take the whale of a lot of Christian prayers to comfort a man who shrank from the jab of a needle.

Later, Magdalena and Sister Augustine came in to change his sheets. Magdalena was small, young, plump, and matter of fact; Augustine was a tall, middle aged, matronly nun, with a soft voice and brown eyes. They knew their job and they did it adroitly, tilting his fourteen stone this way and that and rolling him off the old sheet and onto the new. It was like a conjuring trick. He felt clean, and pampered, and a little ashamed. This was the soft life, and he had not opted for softness. It was luxury, and luxury was no part of the rule. No one had ever made his bed for him before. He had made his own bed and he had lain on it.

"Now we'll remove your screens," said Sister Augustine. "It's high time that you saw where you are and met the rest of the community."

It was a tiny ward with a bed in each corner, and the one on Bernard's left was empty. A man moved slowly across the ward from the bed in the opposite corner. He was a shade over six feet, and he had

51.

heavy jowls and unkempt, greying hair. A shabby dark brown dressing gown was looped about his middle. Red pyjama legs and plaid slippers showed beneath it. He navigated his way carefully, sliding his feet along the floor, and stood beside Bernard's bed.

"You're looking grand today, Brother. How are you feeling?"

"Fair enough," said Bernard.

The big fellow sat down on the bed.

"I'm just three days over an operation myself. Double hernia."

"It doesn't seem to have taken much out of you."

"It's hard to kill a bad thing. And sure nowadays an operation is nothing. Nothing at all. They give you the first injection about half-an-hour before you go up to the theater, and after that you couldn't care less, as the saying is. You get a second injection on the table and Bob's your uncle. You have a little bit of discomfort when you wake up, but it's not worth talking about. I still have the stitches, of course, and about a square yard of plaster. I'm like a baby in a binder."

He patted his middle with a proprietary air.

"My name's Briody," he went on. "Mick Briody. Insurance agent here in the city. Married, and with six children."

Then he lowered his voice.

"Your man in the bed beyond is a farmer from Cavan. Hardly ever opens his trap. I don't like the look of him at all. He eats next to nothing, and anything he does eat comes up again. It doesn't look good."

He pursed his lips and shook his head, giving weight to his prognosis.

"No, I don't like the look of him at all. Give me something that the knife will cure—hernia or appendix. An operation for me every time.

"I'm going to have a shave now," he went on. "It'll freshen me up a bit. Look at me! I'm like a blooming Franciscan."

He started off across the ward again, keeping close to the beds, like a ship hugging the coast. When he got back to the basin beside Bernard's bed he was breathing heavily. "I'm feeling grand," he said as he began to lather, "but a spell in the bed takes it out of a man. I haven't a puff in me."

If he hadn't, he managed bravely without it. He might have been making a general confession. He had a son in the bank, two daughters in the Civil Service, and two sons and a daughter still at school. His eldest brother was an insurance inspector in Harristown, New Jersey. He came home every two years. America, that was where the money was. A man would need to be working for the hell of a long time in Ireland before he could afford a holiday in the States. That was the God's truth.

"My hobby is fishing," he said when he was drying his razor. "It's a grand sport. But maybe I'm tiring you?"

"Not at all," said Bernard.

The big fellow bent down and whispered. "But don't blame me too much, Brother. I was just starved for a bit of chat. Your man over beyond hasn't a word to throw to a dog."

Briody went back to bed, and Bernard began to think about fish.

He thought of the strange, misshapen fish that lived in tropic seas and ocean depths: lop-sided fish and transparent fish and butterfly fish; football jersey fish and striped awning fish; hammerheads and gumboils and bubbleheads.

The Swilly was full of fish: herring and mackerel, gurnet and plaice, pollock and whiting. There were great congers too—as a boy he had seen one of them coiled in a box on Derryleigh pier, and even in death it seemed ready to strike—and leathery, fever spotted dogfish. The dogfish tore great holes in the nets, and the fishermen had no love for them. When they caught one they would cut off its fins and throw it back into the tide, and it would go skittering madly along the surface, half submerged but unable to sink, and doomed to die in frenzy in a familiar element that had turned strange and inimical.

When the fry were in, the crazed mackerel filled the bay and grabbed at anything that moved or shone. There was no need for finesse then. If you had a line in one of the boats that went out from the Kinnegar or Anny you could catch mackerel as fast as you stripped them from the hook, and match their greed with your own.

But in the hill country, herring was king. Mackerel were right enough when the hunger was on you, but the Glen folk put no great *meas* on them. They filled a gap, like plaice and flounders, but herring was king. When Denis Big Kate or Tadhg Anton came up from the shore with creaking carts it was always herring they had with them—limp shining *scadain*, fresh from the salt tide and as cheap as scallions.

Sometimes the herring came close in, maddened and gluttonous, wheeling in shoals on the trail of the fry and fretting the little bay beneath the coast guard station like a shower of hail. When that happened, you had no call to give pennies to

54 .

Denis Big Kate or cadge the loan of a boat from Tadhg Anton. When the herring were in, the news came up from the shore like a rallying cry, and the whole mobile population made for the tide. Men and women, boys and girls, tucked up their skirts and trousers and caught herring in buckets and sieves and tin pandies. The herring went as suddenly as they came, but it was a wild orgy while it lasted, a manna of glistening scales. "An illumination of herring" Old Annie called it once.

The herring were roasted on the red turf, and they were fine feeding. A hungry man, stripping the flesh from them with calloused fingers, might leave eight or ten skeletons on the table before he sighed and reached for his cap. When you had your fill of fresh herring and potatoes and a bowl of buttermilk or strong tea to wash them down, you wouldn't call the king your uncle, and when you rose from the table you were as tight as a drum.

On bright nights, too, when the tide was ebbing and the moon was full, you could dig foot-long silvery sand eels on the wet beach. You struck deep with your spade, and when the spit was turned you stabbed with a sharp knife at the flickering white shadows. For this work you needed to be quick and keen-eyed and supple, for the eels could burrow into the sand again quicker than worms into the sod.

The food that the Glen got from the sea— herring and mackerel, sand eels and shellfish— helped to eke out its porridge and buttermilk, oat cake and potatoes. There were seaweeds too: carrigeen moss that yielded a toothsome, glutinous stuff like blancmange; and a green, cabbage-like weed called sloke. And all this helped to rear tall, tireless mountainy men who labored cold barren fields, and cut turf for firing, and timed each day's work against the darkness. Meat was a luxury that they saw three or four times a year, but they thrived without it. They seldom fattened, but they had big bones and iron muscles, and sore labor was their birthright.

In the Glen, tillage meant unrewarding work in peaty soil that no man would have chosen for husbandry of his own free will. And poor as the soil was, there was not half enough of it. The farms were pitifully small, and the low, wide-based walls that separated the tiny fields one from another were built of loose stones that had been levered out of the cold earth.

In the days of the chieftains, all this had been rough grazing for sheep and the haunt of snipe and curlew. It was not until the long-hoped-for Spanish help had come too late and in the wrong place, and the exiled chiefs had found sanctuary in Rome and Louvain, the the Gael came perforce to the mountains and the moorlands and raised chimney smoke in places which until then had known only hunters' fires.

The Scots moved inland along the banks of the salmon rivers, and the rich valley lands of Ulster were divided into thousand-acre lots by men with maps in their hands and greed in their hearts. Soldiers were given estates against arrears of pay and sold them for the price of a week's drinking to hard-eyed adventurers who became landed gentry overnight. Some of the dispossessed were allowed to remain as laborers on the lands that had been theirs for centuries; the rest became tenants-at-will of tiny holdings in places like the Glen, where they paid crushing rents to absentee landlords and

56 .

tithes to parsons whose services they scorned, and brooded sullenly on ancient wrongs.

The Gael lost the good lands, and he had to fight for the bad. For in time even the tiny fields that he had won from the sterile peat were grudged to him, and the improvements that he had made by his own labor were used as an excuse for raising his rent. If he built a new byre, or moved the midden from his door, or whitewashed the gable wall of his house, he was penalized for his industry, and if he could not meet his rent on gale day his thatch would be set on fire and his walls tumbled; and even before the straw had burnt itself out, the landlord's black cattle would be breast-deep in his unharvested crops.

It was a long fight and a bitter one, and resolute men had to face the eviction squads, pitting scythes against carbines, before side-whiskered men in Westminster advanced the money that enabled the tenants to purchase their holdings and have some measure of security in the fields they had wrought. The farms in the Glen were not worth buying, but they were bought. They were not worth working, but they were worked. The stubborn Gael lived on in a place where a people less tenacious, less wedded to the soil, less inured to hardship, less resigned or less determined, would have foundered and perished.

The Glen was never much above hunger, but it never starved. It had porridge and potatoes, and *scadain* and seaweed; and a man with a cow in the byre and a few sheep on the mountain could feed barefooted children until they were big enough to hire out by the half-year with the strong farmers in the Lagan valley—who were of a different creed and race—or take a reaping hook and two pairs of socks and a burden of oat cake and sail from Derry to help in the saving of Scotland's harvests.

Firing was plentiful. Every house had its turf bank on the mountain, or a slice of inexhaustible moorland, and the old people who were beyond saving their own fuel could always count on a few loads of peat from their neighbors. There might be little in the pot at times, but there was always a good fire for the boiling of it.

Money was the trouble: money for the rent, money for shoe leather, money for tea and flour and Indian corn and pigtail tobacco. A man might sell a few tons of potatoes in October, or make a wheen of pounds on spring lambs or mountain cattle. And the women carried eggs to Manus the Shop, who credited them against tea and snuff and caraway seeds and packed them in crates for Glasgow.

It was hard going, and the end was always the same: the end was the emigrant ship, and the empty hearth, and old doting women sitting their lone and telling their beads.

Bernard knew his lineage and his roots. Six generations before, there had been snug homes along the Foyle and the Shrule and the Bann, in a land where the corn grew high and the cattle had a gloss on them, where men sang songs at night and remembered the golden age of the Gael. Once in a while there would be forays and cattle raids and the taking of hostages, but after every blood-spilling there would be years of plenty.

Bernard knew the story of his race. He had heard it over and over again while he was still young enough to wear the rough homespun skirted frocks that the Glen boys wore before they grew into trousers. He had come from men who had burned the heather and heaved the grey stone and clawed fields out of the side of the mountain—with hatred in their hearts and the memory of green pastures in their nostrils.

4.

The brethren came regularly to visit him, especially Brother Paul and Brother Colman; Paul with his barrel body and cherubic face, Paul who would never be older or wiser; Colman, the quester, grey as a badger, worried and worried looking. He could always see by their faces that the Prior had warned them not to tire him, or excite him, or stay too long. But they didn't send up his blood pressure. They were quiet, restful men. They were his own, and he was glad to have them with him.

Father Austin, too, came regularly. Austin was his theological adviser. He kept him right on questions of dogma. Austin was tall, lean, and bespectacled. He knew Rome like the back of his hand, and he could talk of Mary Major's and San Clemente

60.

and the Via de Santo Quattro as familiarly as other
men might speak of Adam and Eve's or Clanbrassil
Street—but he would rather speak about the Wex-
ford hurling team. He was a Doctor of Canon
Law of the Lateran—*summa cum laude*, they said
—but he still had the fresh look of a novice.

Austin came in early one afternoon.

"How are they all beyond?" said Bernard.

"Threshing. But we want you back soon. Paul's
cooking is a bit sketchy at times."

Trying to please me, he is, thought Bernard.

"Any news?"

"A Brother Hilary was asking for you. He's over
from England for a few days. Not much bigger
than a milk churn. He says he was with you in the
Novitiate."

"So he was. Tiny Tim they used to call him.
He was in St. Michael's for ten years—but that
was before you came to the use of reason. He must
be getting on now, like myself. He's well over
seventy."

Bernard loved all the brethren for Christ's sake
—even the holy ones, who were hardest to live
with—but he liked Hilary. He would not have
swapped him for a whole quiver of theologians.
And he hadn't seen him for donkey's years.

"It was good of you to come, Father Austin."

"You're an old cod, Bernard."

"How so?"

"You're only waiting until I go and Hilary
comes."

"Is he coming?" said Bernard innocently.

"Isn't that what I came in to tell you? And it
was like bringing a bag of sweets to a child. You
brightened up as soon as you heard it."

61 .

"Maybe so, maybe so. It does an old man good to meet another old man. Hilary and I were young once. Now we are like old twisted apple trees."

"Hilary will be here about five," he said. "I'll tell your apple trees you were asking for them."

"Do that, like a good man. Tell them I'll see them before Christmas."

Hilary had changed in twenty years. He seemed to have lost bulk—though he never had had much in the way of bulk. But he was still the same Hilary: tinier than ever; a pocket religious, a friar minimus.

"What happened you at all, Bernard?"

You know, Hilary, you know. You have been well briefed. "A stroke, I think, Hilary, though no one has as much as mentioned the word. They talk about the weather, and they say I'm looking grand and that I'm making good progress, but they never tell me what's wrong with me. But I have a good notion. The old heart isn't as young as it used to be. But tell me, how do you like it over in England?"

"One kitchen is much like another, Bernard, and I don't see much else. I make the meals, and all the others are out gathering money."

"Questing?"

"Have sense, man. Questing wouldn't put a dinge in the money we have to scrounge. We use more modern techniques. We have whist drives and silver circles and sales of work and bob-a-week sweeps and guest teas and Gilbert and Sullivan and carnivals and darts competitions. There's no end to it."

"But what's it for?"

"It's the same all over England. The parishes were always hard up, but now they have to find the money for modern secondary schools and the Lord knows what.

"It gets tiresome after a while," he went on. "We had an old parish priest in doing a retreat about a month ago and you should have heard him. 'The training I got in the seminary didn't fit me for the work I have to do now,' he said. 'They'll have to change the whole course and bring it into line with the times. What a young priest should get now is a year at philosophy, two years at theology, and four years in Chipperfield's Circus.' "

"Talking of parish priests—"

This was from Briody: Briody, propped up in bed behind the newspaper that he had already read from cover to cover and was using as a shield. He had been holding himself back for manner's sake, but now that the conversation had taken a general turn he put down his paper and folded his glasses.

"Talking of parish priests—" he said again.

"This is Brother Hilary," said Bernard. "Brother Hilary, Mr. Briody."

"Pleased to meet you, Brother Hilary. This is one I think you'll enjoy. I knew an old parish priest once—an odd soul if ever there was one, and that doesn't reveal his identity, for some of them are as odd as two left boots."

"Amen to that," said Hilary.

"Well, one day someone asked him if he had a curate living in the house with him. And what does your man say? 'A curate!' says he. 'I wouldn't have one of them for any money. Curates are dirty things to have about a house.'

"But the oddest parish priest I ever met," he went on, "is down in my own place at home. He must be eighty if he's a day, and he'd be hard to beat. When he said last Mass at Carrigban he used to have a cup of tea on the altar before he began to preach, and some of the local women took turns at making it for him. The clerk used to make it at first, but he said the clerk couldn't make proper tea, and then the women took a hand.

"But he wasn't pleased with the women either, and one morning when he had cut the top off his egg he said, 'Do you know what I'm going to tell you? There's not a woman in this parish knows how to boil an egg.' From the altar, mind you! Oh, he was as odd as they come. There wasn't the match of him in the thirty-two counties, nor the beat of him anywhere. But this is the best one of all."

Briody had a fashion of finishing his stories with an option on the next one. He let you know when he paused that it was not for want of ammunition.

"This is the best you ever heard. He has his tombstone in the graveyard for the past twenty years. God's truth! You mightn't believe it, but anyone in the place will bear me out. He has his tombstone ready, and he's as proud of it as another man would be of a racing mare.

"And he has everything filled in on it but the date of his death. Did you ever hear better! All they'll have to do when he goes is to chisel out the figures. And do you know what he has at the very bottom of it?" He looked up like an auctioneer seeking a bid. 'Beloved by his people and especially by the little children,' he has. And then, 'Look for me in the nurseries of Heaven.' "

"He must be an oddity all right," said Hilary.

"Oddity is no name for it, Brother. No name at all. One of the curates said to me one day: 'If he isn't in the nursery, he won't be there at all.' "

Briody had a repertoire of eccentric parish priests, and he was bent on giving a recital, but when Sister Magdalena came in he stopped in his tracks. Magdalena went to the farmer from Cavan and smoothed his pillow. Then she tucked in Briody's coverlet. And all these meaningless movements were full of meaning. She was like a provost marshal on his rounds.

"I hope you're not tiring yourself, Brother, and undoing all our good work?"

"Have sense, woman. I haven't seen this young fellow for over twenty years, and a bit of crack will do both of us good. This is Brother Hilary."

Hilary rose to shake hands with Magdalena. And he stayed on his feet.

"Maybe I should be going?"

"Where would you be going?" said Bernard. "Sure you're barely in. Don't mind Sister Magdalena. She fusses over me like a hen with a sick chicken."

"Well, he can stay for a little while, but not for too long. We have to get you better, you know."

"Och, don't be so persnickety, Sister. Hilary will do me more good than pills and injections."

Magdalena smiled. "Was he always as stubborn as this, Brother Hilary?"

"Always and ever, Sister. He's as headstrong as a mule."

Hilary stayed, but not for long. He was edgy and restless. He kept looking towards the door. "You're not feared of the Sister, are you?" said Bernard. "Her bark is worse than her bite. Tell me, what brought you to Ireland?"

"I came over to my sister's funeral. She's the last of them. I'm bird alone now."

65 .

"When are you going back?"

"In a day or two."

"You'll be in again?"

"If I can, Bernard, but I have a lot of things to see to."

Hilary stayed, and there was a comfort in his nearness, but they had little to say to one another after that. It was like saying good-bye in a railway station, Bernard was thinking.

That evening a new patient arrived. He opened the door gently, and came into the ward as if he feared a booby-trap.

"Good night. Is this ward thirteen?"

"Right first time," said Briody.

The newcomer was a thin, low-sized man who looked in the late sixties and was dressed with shabby formality in a blue serge suit, a stiff, old-fashioned linen collar, and a black woolen tie. His face was sallow, and his watery eyes, peering this way and that through thick lenses, gave him the look of a scared mouse. Asked to place him, you would have guessed that he was a lawyer's clerk who still used a steel pen.

Briody took him in hands at once. Briody was the doyen of the corps.

"Welcome to our humble home. My name's Briody."

"Mine's Patterson. John Patterson."

"This is Brother Bernard."

"How do you do, Brother?"

"And this is Mr. McAllister."

"How do you do, Mr. McAllister?"

The farmer showed no sign that he had heard.

"Are you for the knife, Mr. Patterson?"

66 .

Patterson bowed his head like one awaiting sentence.

"I'm afraid so."

"What's the trouble?"

"An appendix."

"An appendix!" said Briody. "Easiest of the lot. No bother at all. Now a gall bladder would be different, but an appendix is child's play. They take out an appendix here as easily as a dentist takes out a bad tooth. Who's doing you?"

"Dr. Melville."

"You couldn't have a better man. One of the best in Dublin. Bar none. A brilliant man. You're in good hands, Mr. Patterson. He'll have you on your feet again in no time."

Patterson smiled forlornly.

"I hope so."

He began to undress. He took off his coat and vest and put them on a hanger in the press. He unfastened his high collar and rolled his thin tie around his forefinger. He opened his case and laid neatly folded pyjamas on the bed. Everything he did was done slowly and methodically. He might have been getting his books ready for audit.

Briody followed every movement with his eyes and talked in staccato bursts. Patterson said nothing at all. He took off his shirt and woolen undervest showing a chest as flat as an ailing boy's. When he climbed into his bed the bulk of him scarcely showed.

Patterson had the bed on Bernard's left. The little ward was at full strength now. Its four beds were occupied.

"You'll like it here," said Briody. "It's the best hospital in Dublin. Good meals and a grand lot of nuns. Kindness itself, they are. "And I wouldn't worry about an appendix."

"No?" said Patterson.

"Not at all. An operation is child's play these days. Whole technique has been changed. Is this your first operation?"

"It is," said Patterson. "I was never in hospital before, and I'm feeling a bit scared. At my age an operation is always a risk."

"Crossing a street is a risk, if it comes to that— aye, or getting up on a ladder to hang a picture. But look at me—I had a double hernia, and the operation didn't take a feather out of me!"

Bernard was glad that Briody had someone to talk to. He wanted to catch up on his thinking.

5 .

There had been seven children in the house by the burn, five boys and three girls. Bernard was the fifth of them. He had been Brother Bernard for a long, long time, but he had begun life as Pat Logue, one of the Logues of Ardsbeg, the one who came after Tom and Hughie, Kate and Mary, and before Barney and Ellen. There had been two other children, but they had died in infancy.

Bernard began life as Pat Logue, but things might easily have been different. He was born during a spring when many of the Glen infants had died of some strange malady, and the local wiseacres, well versed in *pishoges* and superstitions, recalled an ancient specific and advised expectant mothers that if they wanted their children to survive they should give them names that had never been used before in the family or district. This theory put an interdict on the names that had cropped up in the school roll for generations as inevitably as recurring decimals—names like Pat and Neil and Manus and Brigid and Mary Kate—and brought about a crop of such outlandish names as Stanislaus and Gregory and Cecil and Priscilla and Honoria. The aberration lasted less than a year—a new curate put an end to it—and long after the reason for it had been forgotten it served as a method of checking ages.

Bernard was christened Pat, but the name originally selected for him was Adolphus; and Adolphus he would have been but for his godmother, Maggie Shuvlin of Carrowreagh. Maggie came to the house on the morning of his Baptism, wrapped him in the family christening shawl, and asked by what name he was to seek admittance into the Church.

Then she laid him down on the bed again beside his mother. "No, Nora," she said, "I'll not do it. I'm sib to you, and I'd be glad to bring any wean of your mothering to the priest, but if you're going to call this innocent wee man Adolphus, you can get another godmother for him. I wouldn't have hand, act, or part in giving a wean a name like that. I wouldn't have it on my conscience. Surely there are plenty of good Irish names for you to choose from! And what call have you to be going outside your own family? You've been listening to old gabs like Hughie Edward and Ned Ban. Adolphus indeed! I wouldn't give Adolphus to a dog, much less a Christian!"

Maggie's protest carried the day. For one thing, the Logues had no wish to offend her. For another, it would have been impossible to find a substitute godmother at short notice—and in the circumstances. So they came down from the heights and asked Maggie to pick the name herself.

"No, I'll not," said Maggie. "He's your own child and it's for you to name him."

They might have called him Joachim or Hiram or Jonathan, but they compromised and called him Pat: and Maggie, mollified and glad that she had averted a great wrong, carried him to the church and answered for him at the font. Bernard heard the story many a time from Maggie herself, and he never forgot to pray for the valiant woman who had stood for him—and by him.

Pat Logue got the normal schooling of the Glen. He went to school regularly from harvest to seed-sowing, but only once in a while during the rest of the year: and when he was fourteen he stayed home for good.

He helped his father at the turf-cutting on the mountain. He spread the slimy black sods for drying, he "footed them" and built them into little ricks, and when the sun and the wind had put a skin on them, he ferried them home day after day with a panniered donkey that followed the twisting mountain pads and was often up to its shoulders in the tough-rooted heather.

At spraying time he mixed bluestone and white soda in the big stained barrel, and when his back was strong enough to bear the metal knapsack he walked up and down the drills, working the lever with one hand and squirting the fine blue spray on to the white blossoms with the other. He "rodded" corn for the scythesman, holding back the grain with a long sally rod so the crunching blade would have clearance to shear in near the ground and leave a low stubble: and sometimes he girdled the fallen swathes and piled them in pyramids one against the other.

He cleaned the byre and the stable, and trundled the dung to the midden. After the hay was cut, he herded the cows in the stubble and kept them from straying into the corn or potatoes. When the cows were grazing in the hill parks—the moist, sea-green fields that marked the beginning of the heather—he drove them home in the gloaming, put chains about their necks in the byre, and, if the women were otherwise engaged, took his turn at the milking.

In time he learned how to handle horses, and when first Tom, and then Hughie, left home, he began to do more and more of the heavier farm work. By the time he was seventeen he could handle a plough, keeping his furrows straight and turning deftly at the headlands, and he could put an edge on a scythe and mow with a smooth easy rhythm from morning till night.

Anthony Logue, the man of the house, had wrought hard in his day, but rheumatism had stiffened his limbs and made him old before his time. As his sons grew up, he ceded the heavier work to them in their turn. But that was all he ceded. All the decisions were his, and his word was law. He determined the crop rotation and the time for selling young calves and bonhams, and the corn was never ripe for cutting until he had given his decision.

He gave his orders gently and obliquely. "I was thinking," he would say casually, "that maybe you would earth up the spuds in Pairc Mhor the morra," or "It might be no harm if you thought of starting the ploughing on Monday."

He was a quiet, slow-spoken man, with the face

and mind of a scholar. He had a great store of hero tales and traditional stories, and he would walk five miles to hear a new one—he gathered and memorized them long before an interest in them became fashionable. He was not a man of action, or of strong feelings, but he had a great interest in politics, and the neighbors would gather in at night to hear him read political speeches from the newspapers and comment on the doings of the Irish Party at Westminster.

The Logues' farm was a small one, but smallness was not its worst defect. On the map, it measured fourteen Irish acres, but a Meath farmer would not have taken them for four of his own. It grew good potatoes and turnips, but the corn that came from it was stunted and spindly. It was cold, hungry land.

The mountains, which had impoverished the Glen, were in a sense the saving of it. They gave it firing the year round, and rough pasture for the cows, and sweet cropping for the sheep.

The cows got most of their meat on the mountain, where they grazed in the green parks that separated the tillage lands on the lower slopes from the beginnings of peat and heather. But they were herded at times on the roadside, and when the hay was cut they munched the sweet under-grass of the meadows and came home to the byres with swinging udders. The sheep lived on the higher slopes or on the summit, and fared for themselves. Every family in the Glen had its flock of sheep. Their meat brought in badly needed money, and their wool was carded and spun into the making of skirts and trousers and grey, sweat-soaking shirts.

The Logues were poor, but no poorer than their neighbors. Indeed by local standards they were

73 .

comfortably off. They had a horse and a couple of cows. They had food and firing and shelter, and they never went to bed hungry.

They lived in a whitewashed mud cabin that had thick walls, a thatched roof, and a floor of cracked and irregular flags that extended a yard or so into the "street." The main door was seldom shut, except at night and in very stormy weather, but the half-door kept out the stringy fowl and the heavy-keeled geese.

There was a tiny porch—it was really only half a porch, for one side of it was open and led directly into the kitchen—and to the right of it lay the apartment that was known as "the room." The room had a scrubbed table covered with oilcloth, a clock and two white china dogs on the mantel-piece, pictures of the Blessed Virgin and Robert Emmet, a dark brown press, four wooden chairs, and two curtained beds against the back wall. The room was a gesture, a boast to the world. The priest was received there when he called, and a visiting relative once in a blue moon, but that was all. The kitchen was for life and living, but the room was a thing apart. Its clock ticked all day long but there was no one to listen, and the china dogs with their black eyebrows and gold lacing had the place to themselves.

There was always a chill in the room, but the kitchen was warm with life. It was the heart of the house. It was where the family cooked and ate and sat and talked. It was sitting room and bedroom and meeting place. Its day began at rising time and finished only after the Rosary was said at night.

Tucked into the upper right-hand corner of the kitchen and against the wall that separated it from the room (the room was sometimes called "the lower room," because it was on a slightly lower level than the kitchen) was a four-poster bed that stretched in under the loft and was curtained off during the day, giving the effect of a room within a room. The loft was for gear and lumber. It held baskets and pieces of harness, hay rakes and the spraying knapsack and fishing rods, and an old shotgun for scaring the crows.

Opposite the loft and the four-poster bed was a big recessed fireplace sunk into the mouth of a wide chimney. The fire burned night and day, summer and winter. It was an everlasting fire. It was raked over every night, and in the morning, when the grey ash was blown off, there were red living embers underneath to light the pieces of fresh turf that boiled the kettle for the breakfast.

It was always twilight in the kitchen, except near the tiny, deep-silled window above the scrubbed deal table, and in the porch, where the light coming in over the half-door shone on the dresser with its blue-and-red rimmed bowls, white jugs, brown tea-pots, and its necklace-rows of eggs. Light came in too through a small window in the back wall of the kitchen, but it was shadowed by the dark mass of the mountain. It was always twilight in the kitchen, but there was no gloom there, and the general impression was one of cheeriness. The fire glowed all day long as brightly as the fire in a smithy, and over it was the wide whitewashed throat of the chimney, coated thickly with shiny soot.

To one side of the fire and stretching over it was a right angle of blackened metal. From the horizontal arm, which could be swung outwards on the hinge of the upright, hung an iron chain to the rings of which pots and pans could be hooked. When the potatoes were beginning to burst their coats, or when a scone of bread was nicely browned, the woman of the house swung the horizontal arm outwards, lifted the utensil from the chain with her hand wrapped in her skirt, and set it down on the eggshaped stones of the hearth.

At the back of the kitchen and opening off it was the tiny "upper room," which stood out from the house in a sentry-box bulge. It was the only one of its kind in the Glen: all the other houses were two room cottages without additions or trimmings. The upper room was where the great crock of cream was kept. It was a cool place, away from the heat of the kitchen and in the shadow of the mountain.

The construction of the Glen houses was simple. They had no plumbing, no brickwork, no staircases, no complexities. But their thick mud walls kept them warm in winter and cool in summer, and their snug wigs of thatch held firm against the sudden gusts that swept through the corridors of the hills.

The potato was the basic food of the Glen; and in every house for miles about a great pot of potatoes was boiled every day. In the Glen, potatoes meant dinner, and dinner meant potatoes. When the potatoes were boiled in their skins they would be peeled at the table, dipped in salt, and washed down with buttermilk. But usually they were peeled egg-white before going into the pot, and then, after boiling and draining, pounded with a heavy beetle until they were as fine as sifted flour. Great mounds of potatoes were piled on each

76 .

plate, and a crater was made in the middle to hold a nugget of butter. This dish was known as "champ," and it was fine feeding, especially when it was laced with pieces of onion or young scallions.

The smaller, marble-sized potatoes were boiled and given to the pigs, or mixed with meal and fed to the hens. In the economy of the Glen, the potato was a vital factor.

Tea was taken morning and evening and after dinner. It was strong black tea, for the Glen folk always bought the best leaf—this was their only extravagance. With the tea went long thick slices of homemade scone. The scones were baked on the pan over the kitchen fire, and they were almost as big as bicycle wheels. When a woman was slicing a scone of bread, she held it against her breast like a big drum and sliced inwards towards her neck.

Oaten stirabout, or "brohan," was sometimes taken for breakfast, and always for supper. In every house in the valley the brohan snored and bubbled all evening in a black, three-legged pot, and it was moved up to a higher ring of the chain when it was well cooked. It was thick wholesome stuff, and when it cooled it was as solid as blancmange. Sometimes it was made from maize or "Indian buck," which had been introduced during the famine days. Sometimes, too, scones would be made from maize, or a few handfuls of "yellow meal" would be mixed in to flavor the oat bread.

When a Glensman wanted his supper he rose from his place at the fire, took a bowl from the dresser, half filled it with sweet milk or buttermilk, and added spoonfuls of brohan from the pot. Then he took a drink of "clean water" from the

6.

It was a bright, frosty morning. The sun sparkled through the window panes and filled the ward with light. It was a bright, frosty morning, and Patterson, the new patient, was for the knife.

Dr. Kerrigan, the house surgeon, came in shortly after nine to give him his preliminary injection and briefing. Kerrigan was small and boyish looking, quiet-spoken and apologetic.

"This won't hurt in the slightest," he said as he charged the syringe. "You may feel your mouth a little dry after a while, but that's quite normal. We'll be taking you up to the theater about ten."

Kerrigan went, and his assistant took over.

It was Briody's hour. "You won't feel a thing, Mr. Patterson. They'll have that appendix out of you as easy as winking. And that first injection is

79.

powerful stuff. It leaves you as relaxed as a kitten. You'll be that drowsy after half-an-hour or so that if they told you they were going to remove your kidneys instead of your appendix you wouldn't give a damn."

Patterson could have done with a little relaxing. He looked frightened and woebegone.

Briody stretched himself luxuriously in the bed, raising the clothes at the bottom with his toes, and resting his neck in the nest of his fingers. He was warming up.

"When they come for you" (he made it sound like an execution) "you'll be as wide awake as you are now, and when they wheel you into the theater you'll know everything that's happening to you, but you won't care a continental damn. That's what the first injection will do for you. And when you get the final shot on the table, Bob's your uncle. You'll go out like a light and they can rip away at you . . . How are you feeling?"

"Jiggy enough. I never had an operation before, you know."

"What about it? Neither had I, until I got my hernia done. There's always a first time."

"I wish it was all over," said Patterson.

The escort party arrived: two nuns, Nurse Harty and Michael, the houseboy, in his short white coat. Patterson's feet were encased in thick white socks, which gave a sacrificial touch to the proceedings. He was slid out of bed onto the trolley, covered with blankets, and wheeled off. When he had gone his bed seemed horribly empty.

"He's a bit shook," said Briody. "I did what I could to cheer him up."

"You did," said Bernard.

"But I was wasting my breath. I don't think he

even heard me, he was that scared. In a way, of course, you could hardly blame him. Sure he hasn't a pick on him. He's as thin as a sparrow in February. He would have been the better of a bit of building up, but I suppose there was no time. You can't take chances with an appendix."

He sounded like a meeting of the College of Surgeons.

"I wouldn't give much for his heart either," he went on. "I don't like the color of him one bit."

"These thin fellows are often wiry enough," said Bernard.

Briody considered this second opinion.

"I grant you that, Brother. It's a good point. But there's nothing like a bit of meat on a man's bones when he goes on the table. Unless of course you have a regular porter belly—saving your presence, Brother. Doctors don't like to operate when a man has a belly on him like a drowned sheep. But they like to have something to cut into. Still, you never know. And there's very few dies on the table in these days. Besides, Melville is a right good surgeon."

He was giving Patterson an outside chance.

"It's a big change from the old days," he said then. "Yes, there have been great improvements in surgery. There was a time when all they did was to give a man a quietener of whiskey, stick a plug of wood in his mouth so that he would have something to bite on, get a couple of fellows to hold him down, and then saw off his leg."

"I heard of a doctor who cut off his own leg," said the farmer from Cavan.

Briody looked like a lecturer who had been interrupted by one of his students.

"His own leg!"

"That's what I said."

"I don't believe it."

"Well, you may then. I read it in the paper."

"Where did it happen?"

"I don't know. But I read it."

"Sure he would bleed to death!"

"He didn't," said the farmer. Presently he added, as if he were producing irrefutable evidence, "He was an Australian."

"You can't believe all you read in the papers," said Briody.

The farmer said nothing more. He had said his piece, and he had nothing to add. And he did not speak again for several days.

Briody swung his legs out of the bed and scratched his poll vigorously with both hands.

"The sooner I get these stitches out the better. That damn surgeon of mine was to have been in yesterday to give me the all clear. It's the divil's own job getting into your trousers when you feel like a bag of cement."

He took his shirt, socks, and trousers out of the press and began to dress himself slowly. Then he walked across the ward to the wash basin. He washed with a great splashing and gurgling, and soused his hair before he made a parting in it.

A thought struck him then.

"Do you know what I'm thinking? Patterson has been a fair time away. God grant he's all right. I wouldn't like anything to happen to the poor fellow. You never know what you'll find when you open a man up. You just never know. I think I'll take a turn up the corridor and see if there's any word of him."

He finished his dressing quickly and went out.

The farmer cleared his throat noisily. After that the ward was very quiet.

Patterson came back, stiff as a mummy. He was wheeled in on the trolley, lifted into bed, and banked with hot water bottles. He was alive, but Bernard had never seen any living person who looked so dead.

A nun sat by his bedside, knitting and waiting; waiting for the return of the real Patterson, the one who spoke and moved, who made entries in ledgers, and folded his tie round his index finger every night. In the meantime, something that was only bulk and weight and strange noises had to be watched lest it should choke with phlegm or need oxygen or a blood-drip. The nun sat like a mother watching over a sick child. Now and again she would slap his cheek gently and call his name.

Bernard was thinking of life and death; of this suspended life that was the image of death; of the dignity and pity and mystery of it all. Vessels and conduits, noises and movements—these things were not life but the trappings and symptoms of life. Life was not localized, or finite, or subject to corruption. You could lose a hand, or a leg, or your reason, and still have life. You could lie inert like Patterson, seeing nothing, hearing nothing, knowing nothing, and still have life. Death was the sundering of a partnership. It was like a flitting or an eviction. The body crumbled and decayed when its time came; and its time came when it lost its tenant.

"Wake up, Mr. Patterson! Wake up! Can you hear me? Wake up, wake up!" The nun's voice was louder now; unwearied, insistent, summoning. Patterson was fighting back. He groaned and muttered. His hands moved a little. He opened his eyes and shut them again.

"That's better, Mr. Patterson. Can you hear me? Wake up, Mr. Patterson."

Patterson muttered inarticulately, and there was a new quality in his breathing. He was not back yet, but he was on the threshold.

Briody had been sitting in a chair reading. He crossed the ward and sat down on Bernard's bed.

"He's over it now," he said.

"Yes, thank God," said Bernard.

"I had a feeling he would make it."

"Where is he from, I wonder?"

"Dublin, where else? Wouldn't you know by his accent? A born Jackeen. You couldn't mistake them. I'm a Roscommon man myself. From near Ballaghadereen, where the good mutton comes from."

"Are you long out of it?"

"Over thirty years . . . You're from the north, I'm thinking?"

"Aye."

"And far up, too?"

"As far up as you could go without getting your feet wet. I'm from Donegal."

"A poor county," said Briody. "There isn't much of a living in it."

"Poor enough," said Bernard.

We raised men, not mutton, he was thinking. We peopled the world. We have suburbs as far away as Brooklyn and Philadelphia. I come from a poor county, but I wouldn't swap it for ten Roscommons and an illumination of fat sheep.

There was a tradition of scholarship in the Glen. It had been nourished by the old hedge-schoolmasters who had travelled up and down the country, spending a month here and a month there, and teaching the children of a district in return for board and lodging and such silver as the people could scrape together. Some of them were spoiled priests who still remembered their Latin and Greek; some were roistering poets whose Gaelic verses, larded with classical allusions, were preserved in yellowing manuscripts or in the tenacious memories of a people who saw in them part of the heritage that the plantations had fouled and impoverished. In an age when education was forbidden to all except those who were willing to swallow the reformed doctrines as the price of it, the hedge-schoolmasters kept the tradition of scholarship alive, handing on a flicker of the flame that had blazed in Clonard and Clonmacnoise and from which the lamps of western Europe had once been rekindled.

The Glen boys left school early, but many of them came back to it when they were sprouting side-whiskers and tried to find room for their long mountainy legs under desks that seemed to have shrunken since they left them. They came back to school in the long winter nights, and of their own volition, partly because of an inherited urge, and partly to fit themselves for the emigrant ship. They wanted to get away from the mountain lands, and they wanted to have something with them when they went.

The curriculum of Master Friel's night school ranged from long division and simple interest to English history and mensuration and Latin roots. It answered the needs of those who wanted to strengthen their literacy against the time when they would sail to Glasgow or Philadelphia, and of those whose ambition was to stay at home and wear the dark uniform of the Royal Irish Constabulary. The latter-day scholars paid the Master threepence a week (his official salary from the Department of Education was fifty-six pounds a year, paid quarterly) and each of them dropped a few sods of turf in the corner of the porch as he came in.

Bernard went to the night school in his turn and learned the rivers of India and the shires of England, square root and compound interest, parsing and analysis. He wrote essays on "Procrastination is the Thief of Time," and "Thrift," and "The Lessons of History." He linked "pes" with "pedal" and "miles" with "military" and "corpus" with "corporal." He learned the importance of Aden and Singapore and Gibraltar, and the achievements of Wellington and Nelson—names like these being singled out for attention because they were much more likely to crop up in the Police Entrance Examination than Aileach or Vinegar Hill, Wolfe Tone or Napper Tandy.

His post-primary education did not take him very far, but it filled some gaps in his mind and it helped to pass the dark winter evenings. It was purposeful, practical, factual. It might fit a man for the barrack square of the Constabulary Depot in the Phoenix Park, but it fed no dreams. It was a matter of words and symbols, of tabulated facts, of black marks on white paper, and there was a side of the mind that it did not touch at all.

Master Friel did what he could, did it well, and Bernard was grateful to him. But he had another tutor to whom he was more deeply indebted. It was Father Dan who fired his imagination and furnished his mind with things that were outside the gift of the old *Sixth Book* and *Sullivan's Arithmetic* and the *Spelling Book Superseded*.

Father Dan McGonigal was a stocky man, broad in the shoulders and with a tremendous neck. He had a wide face, a deep, wrinkled forehead, and full lips. There was a look of strength about him, and his white, curly hair had changed color long before its time. His eyes were his most striking feature. They were dark, brooding eyes, shaded by matted, coal-black eyebrows.

He was a first cousin of Mrs. Logue's, and a curate in Templecarrick, on the far side of the Lough. He came to the Glen for a few days several times a year, and he always spent part of his holidays there. The rest he spent with his brother Colm, who was a publican in Glasgow.

They had been reared in Tamney, on the shores of Mulroy Bay, the islanded inlet on the far side of the hill, but the house of their rearing had been derelict for a long time. There were holes in the thatch, and grasping briars round the sunken walls, and all who had lived there, with the exception of Dan and Colm, were under the sod. Consumption had carried them off one after another, and taken its time about it. But before that, Colm had gone to Glasgow to wash bottles in a public house, and Dan had gone to Salamanca for his priesting.

At times Bernard fancied that he could see Father Dan's family history in his eyes, and read there the story of the scutching that had come to the house by Mulroy. But Father Dan's moodiness had a wider background than this, though it was a long time before Bernard knew it.

Sometimes Father Dan would send word that he

was coming, and Micky Anton, who owned one of the three sidecars in the Glen, would go up to Derryleigh to meet him. But usually he came unannounced, crossing the Lough by the rickety paddle-boat, the *Lake of Shadows*, and hiring a sidecar on the quay to take him the rest of the way. He travelled light, bringing his linen and night clothes in a black leather bag shaped like a rolled military ground sheet, but he was always burdened with books.

The Logues had a poor way on them for keeping visitors, for the few beds they had were well tenanted, so when Father Dan came to the Glen he slept in Master Friel's (the Master had a spare bedroom now that his only son had gone to the States) and took his meals with his kinsfolk. A fire would be lit for him in the lower room, and he would be happy there with his books and papers.

He was fond of fishing in the Big Burn, and he had a rod that he had bought in Glasgow and thought the world of. But he was a poor fisherman. He was too restless, too impatient, too highly strung. He was a poor fiddler too. He often borrowed Master Friel's fiddle, but he had no skill in handling it, and no patience to learn.

Reading was his passion. He read quickly and incontinently, with a finger always ready to turn the page, and a tense look on his wrinkled face. When he was tired of reading, he walked. He might be away for hours at a time, going inland over Croc Ard by the moorland road and following the Lough shore from the Saltpans to Derryleigh, or crossing the dark mass of Croc Eala, the Hill of the Swan, by the heather pads, and dropping down then into the Kingdom of Fanad and the shores of Mulroy. Usually he walked slowly and heavily,

88 .

but on these expeditions he carried a stout stick and moved with great strides, like a pilgrim hurrying to reach a hostel before dark. He had a lined cloak with great brass clasps, and at times he would swing it about his throat and over his shoulder, Moorish fashion. It was a trick he had learned in Salamanca.

He was given to spells of silence, but once he started to talk he would go on and on, like a man communing with himself. When Father Dan was in residence, the children watched the door of the lower room at night and prayed that he would not stay at his books until bedtime. The opening of the room door was like the raising of a theater curtain.

Father Dan would stop at the dresser and give a salutation in Irish, which was his native tongue. Then he would cross the kitchen and take the chair that was set for him almost in the angle of the chimney. Father Dan smoked thick plug tobacco, and he always began by paring a pipeful of it into the palm of his hand, slowly and in silence. Then he would sit as if he were meditating a text, his strong face lit and shadowed by the glow of the fire, and his big curved pipe hanging over his chin.

If he was not in the mood for talking he would sit like a brooding Napoleon, sucking at his pipe and saying next to nothing. There was no flow of small talk in him. He either talked or kept silence. But when he talked he opened his heart.

Often he talked of Spain: of the great clanking trains that went down from Paris to Bayonne, and then nosed their way round the western flank of the Pyrenees to Hendaye and the frontier, where you changed to the wider gauge that brought you to Irun and San Sebastian and Valladolid, and on

89 .

then to Medina del Campo, where you changed for Salamanca. He spoke of the cold winters on the high Meseta, and of the glory of spring in New Castile.

There were few asides in his talks, for he was not given to explanations or footnotes, and he never retraced his steps to see if you were following. He spoke of how the morning sun lighted up up the steeple of the Clericia, as if the name were familiar to all his hearers, and when he spoke of the ancient walled city of Ciudad Rodrigo, standing high above the plain and the twisting river, he made no concessions to folk who had never been further than Derry and knew less about the Peninsular War than an ax-head does about snipe shooting. He would spin history into a litany of proper names—Avila and Toledo, Teresa and Saint John of the Cross—and look into the fire with far-away eyes.

It was all meat and drink to Bernard, though he understood only a tithe of it. He gave himself up to the spell of distant places. He felt the hot sun of Castile and listened to the song of the women washing clothes on the banks of the Duero. And the spell was still with him after more than sixty years. When he closed his eyes, Father Dan was still in the chair by the fire and his quick, eager voice was the only sound in the big kitchen.

Father Dan was a partisan. His likes and dislikes were fixed and forever. And he was a Salamanca man to the core.

"The Maynooth men are inclined to be narrow, and the Romans to be proud, but Salamanca broadens a man and humbles him at the same time. It shows him his roots, and teaches him his history. The College of the Irish Nobles—that's what they call it. They honored our race, and our exiled chiefs, and they honor us still. What country did we look to in the dark days? What country sent us guns and men and money? I know that the help was often too long delayed, and that our soldiers ate their hearts out waiting for it, but we must not blame the Spaniards too much. They had their own troubles, and they were watching bigger moves on the draft board of Europe. But what they did they did willingly and generously, and we must never forget it to them.

"The scholars say that the first colonists who came to Ireland came from Spain, and I think they have the rights of it. When you talk to a Spaniard you get to grips with his mind. They are happy and sad by turns, like ourselves. They like singing and dancing, eating and drinking. We must all come from the same stock."

When he closed his eyes, he was a student again. He might have been reading from an old diary.

"We were lonely at first, God help us. Most of us had never been beyond our own parish until we crossed the sea. We used to walk round the quadrangle at night and talk about Ireland, and a letter from home would be read a dozen times. But little by little it came part of us and we became part of it. It did three things for us. It made men of us, and it made priests of us, and it made us Europeans."

7.

Most nights during the rest of the year, some of the neighbors would drop in after dark—for Logue's was a "raking house"—and there would be talk of Glasgow and Boston and Philadelphia, of foundries and public houses, stockyards and rail tunnels. But these were familiar themes. Half the Glen had kin in Philadelphia, and a man who had been no further than Glasgow was regarded as little better than a stay-at-home. Salamanca was different. It was a name in a fairy story. It was Samarkand and Stambol. It had no connection with navvying on the permanent way, or furnace stoking, or Clyde lodging houses.

To listen to Father Dan was to get away from the fireside small talk of crops and cattle, to break away from the confined, mountain-rimmed world of the Glen, from the reek of the smoke, and the somber moorlands, and the eternal knitting of grey socks.

No one ever interrupted him, or changed the subject, or put in a comment of his own. The man of the house might ask a question once in a while, but that was all. The neighbors never obtruded themselves. They would as soon have interrupted the vested priest on the altar. They sat with crossed legs and folded arms, or leaned forward in their seats like the audience at a play.

The creak of a chair or the rasp of a heavy boot might mark the end of a paragraph. But nobody spoke. The woman of the house worked at her knitting, sitting close to the candle (there was an oil lamp on the chimney breast, but it gave poor light for close work), and using a hairpin occasionally to poke smuts from the bowl of melted wax.

Left to himself, Father Dan might stray a little at times and speak of things too deep for his audience. But Anthony Logue could steer him back on course by asking him what Salamanca looked like, or about its two cathedrals: and Father Dan was so full of his subject, and so willing to talk about it, that he never noticed the shepherding.

He said the same thing dozens of times in different ways.

"A golden city, with walls and buildings that seem soaked in the sun. A city of towers and churches and scholars. Half the learning of Europe is there. History and art and architecture. A lovely city. Its fame goes back past Roman times to the very dawn of history. It is one of the glories of Christendom." He always drew back a little then.

"Don't misunderstand me. There's no place like Ireland. It's the finest country on God's green earth. But I loved Salamanca, and sometimes when I think of it the great loneliness is on me. I have never been back to it since I left it, but if God spares me I'll see it again."

There was another loneliness on him too, though it was long afterward before Bernard could put a name on it. Father Dan could sit at times without moving or speaking, but he was never relaxed. There was no quietness in the man. He was like a coiled spring.

At each visit, Father Dan called on Father McLoughlin in the big, bare, tree-hidden house below the chapel. But they were only courtesy calls. He and Father McLoughlin were guest and host. They had little in common except their office.

Father McLoughlin was a quiet, reserved man. He had a weak chest and was scared of his health. He wore heavy underwear and a heavy overcoat, and he went to bed early. He was a lonely priest in a lonely parish, and he liked it that way. He did his work, and served his people, and said his prayers. But he never scraped on a fiddle, or fished in the Big Burn, and he had no memories of Salamanca.

Father Dan said Mass at nine o'clock every morning, and Bernard served him. He was much quicker than Father McLoughlin, and there was a different tune to his Latin—even on the altar he was a Salamanca man. His movements were quick and graceful, and when he turned to give a blessing his vestments skirted about him. But he slowed down always when he drew near the Consecration, and he never hurried the crisis.

On these week mornings there would be very few in the chapel. Old Murt Dunleavy, the Navy pensioner would be there, and a few wrinkled old women telling their beads for all the world to hear, and the Master's wife would come in from the

94 .

school and kneel in the back seat, having left one of the bigger scholars standing on the dyke to watch for an inspector's sidecar coming slowly down the side of Croc Ard. There were no distractions, as there would be at a Sunday Mass: no scraping of heavy boots on the stone floor, no waves of coughing, no rattle of coins. On mornings like these, Bernard felt very close to Father Dan.

And at night, before Father Dan left for the Master's, he would bespeak his acolyte for the morrow. "Nine o'clock in the morning, lad," he would say, plucking at Bernard's cheek with his thumb and forefinger.

It was always late when he left, and he took a bowl of brohan before he went. He ate his supper standing, half filling a bowl with sweet milk and spooning the thick stirabout into it from the pot. Then he would put on his heavy cloak with its great brass clasps, and take a dab of Holy Water from the font on the side of the dresser, and the man of the house would put on his cap and leave him as far as the head of the street.

Afterward, when Anthony Logue came back, took his beads from the nail on the wall, and flopped on his knees to begin the Rosary, the children found it hard to keep their minds on their prayers. Their thoughts were far away, and often they had to be elbowed back to reality when it was their turn to say a decade.

Father Dan was always in a great flurry leaving; and his packing, sketchy as it was, was invariably left to the last minute. It was always the same. Micky Anton's sidecar would be at the door, and Micky himself would be assessing his chances of getting to the town in time to catch the morning boat from Derryleigh and muttering "What on earth is keeping him? You'd think it was to the States he was going!" But Father Dan would still be fussing about, gathering his belongings in his own haphazard fashion with half the house dancing attendance on him. He left socks in Master Friel's, and books and papers everywhere. Something was always missing at the last minute: pipe or breviary or nightshirt or razor. He never left completely, for the sidecar would be no sooner gone than something of his would be found under his pillow, or on the window sill of the lower room, or on the settle in the kitchen.

If he left something important, like his breviary, Jimmy the Post would bring it up to Derryleigh later in the day and it would be sent across to Sard Point by the evening boat. But incidentals like books and papers were held till his next coming, unless he wrote for some of them to be posted to him. They formed a permanent bridgehead, and one that increased with the years.

These books of Father Dan gave Bernard new notions of the outside world. The picture of Europe in his mind's eye became something very different from the dead and faded map, scoured by many a pointer and finger nail, that hung on the schoolroom wall. Little by little it became a living frieze of peoples and cities. And as he grew older he began to have vague notions of studies beyond mensuration and square root, of subjects that got at the basis of thought itself, that linked all created things with each other, and everything with God.

He had something to think about now on dark winter nights by the fire, or when he lay in bed under a patchwork quilt and listened to the wind in the rowans, and the plash of the Big Burn, and the distant thunder of the Atlantic on the headland below the coast guard station.

Until now, his mind had been shaped and formed by the traditions of the Glen and of the religion that hunted men had cherished in it. They were rich traditions, but now they were broadened and widened. Now he saw for the first time that Ireland was Europe and that it had links with Rome and Vienna and Santiago; that it was not a lost and lonely place hidden from all that mattered by the bulk and might of England, and that it was known and honored throughout the length and breadth of the continent to which in its time it had given saints and scholars and fighting men.

Knowledge of this kind was not to be had in the school curriculum of the Glen, which was concerned largely with the history and achievements of an empire which, unlike those of Greece and Rome, would last for ever. Even the reading matter had an imperial bias, and children who were being reared for the emigrant ship spelt their way laboriously through the trial of Warren Hastings, the march of Hyder Ali, and the relief of Lucknow.

Against all this could be set the traditions of the fireside and the stories of an ancient people; the names of missionaries who had sailed up the Loire and the Rhine, and of mighty chiefs who had won renown in the armies of France and Spain, or gone on pilgrimages to Rome, or corresponded in Latin with Louvain and Salamanca. But between the distant past and the grim present, like a great curtain, rose the memories of the immediate past—of defeat and banishment and servitude—that tended to make these ancient glories as dim and unreal as the legendary tales of Finn and Oisin.

But they came to life again with Father Dan. When he talked he could quote chapter and verse. He could speak familiarly of Brest and Toledo, and of St. Gall and Bobbio; Columbanus was as real to him as Owen Roe, and he knew the footsteps of his race from Burgundy to Andalusia and from the Seine to the Danube.

8 .

Before Bernard was seventeen, the family had begun to scatter. Tom, the eldest, was a laborer in one of the Clyde shipyards, and Kate, who came next, was a clerk in a Glasgow provision store. Kate earned little more than her keep, but never a month passed without Tom sending money home to the Glen. He had got away, but he was still tethered. He lived in a Clydeside lodging house, but he was still under a thatched roof in the Glen.

The money he sent home was hard-earned, but he did not grudge it, for he knew the help that his few shillings would be. Besides, thrift was in his blood. It was part of his rearing. Tom was a rock of sense. He was hard-working, solid, and conscientious.

Hughie, the second eldest son, who took his place

when he went, was different. Hughie went with his mother's side of the house, and he had her heart. He had her heart, and he broke it.

He was tall, well-built, and good-looking, and his thick curly hair had a reddish tint to it. He had been a wild one always. He had no love for books, and he had been a sore trial to Master Friel. Hughie seemed to grow up overnight. Even before he left school he was playing for the Glen football team, and he was almost man size even then.

He began to drink when he was only sixteen, and when he was still a week from his eighteenth birthday he came home drunk from Derryleigh Regatta. It was easy getting drink in the Glen, for some of the Meentagh men had stills in the mountain, and you could buy poteen for next to nothing.

There was no viciousness in Hughie, but he was given to roistering and late hours. He would walk five miles to a card game or a dance and come home in the small hours.

His father raved and stormed, but his mother pleaded for him and hid his failings as best she could. She knew the wild streak that was in him, and she knew where it came from.

When Tom went to Glasgow, Hughie took his place on the farm. He did the ploughing and harrowing, and led peats from the moss, and cleaned the stable and byre. Work was no trouble to him, and no day was too long, but once night fell he went his own way.

Hughie slept with Bernard and Barney in the big bed in the lower room, and often they would waken hours after the family had gone to bed and hear him fumbling at the hasp of the half-door and the labored breathing of him as he took off his heavy boots in the porch. If he was lucky, there

100 .

would be silence after that, and he would creep down to the room, let his clothes fall off him where he stood, and tumble into bed. But as often as not they would hear their father's angry mutterings from the bed in the kitchen, and their mother saying "Whisht, Andy, whisht." The poor woman did her best to keep the peace, but the tension grew and grew.

Now and again Andy's patience would break and he would jump out of bed and deliver a lecture from the room door. The burden of it was always the same: "I'm giving you a warning, boy. If you can't come home to this house sober and in good time you can clear to hell out of it."

Hughie would come home early for a night or two after these explosions, and kneel with the others for the family Rosary, but his good resolutions never lasted very long. And in the end he did clear out. When he was nineteen he left home for good, taking nothing with him but the clothes on his back and a clean shirt. No one knew that he was going, and no one knew where he went. He kept his own counsel.

Six weeks later, word came that he was in Liverpool. But the news didn't come from Hughie himself. Hughie never wrote a scrap. He made a clean break.

His going brought a silence to the house. Andy Logue looked into the fire at night, smoking his pipe and keeping his thoughts to himself. Nora stirred the porridge, and knitted socks, and caught pots in her apron to lift them from the fire; and when she said her decade of the Rosary her voice had heartbreak in it, and hope. Her nights were better than her days, for she could go to sleep at night telling herself that Jimmy the Post would surely have a letter in the morning. But when Jimmy passed and brought no word there was nothing in front of her but another long day of waiting.

Hughie left home when he had finished the sowing of the potatoes, which usually began after St. Patrick's Day. Father Dan came to the Glen in October. He had not been there since February, and it was his longest absence. He wrote that he was coming, and Micky Anton went up to Derryleigh to meet him. Bernard was the first to see the flicker of the oil lamp on the sidecar coming down Croc Ard. Ten minutes later he heard the sound of the hooves and the crunch of the wheels on the street.

Father Dan came into the kitchen, wrapped in his great cloak.

"It's grand to be back," he said.

But there was no resilience in his voice, and there was a great weariness in his eyes.

Father Dan usually travelled light, but this time he had a big corded trunk, and a leather suitcase, and two boxes of books (which was as much as Micky Anton's sidecar could carry); and the following day more luggage came down from Derryleigh. It was more like a flitting than a visit.

And now, instead of sleeping in the Master's, he occupied one of the beds in the lower room. This put a strain on the sleeping arrangements, and for the time being Bernard and Barney had to sleep in the kitchen, Bernard in the settle, and Barney stretched on two chairs.

They had been warned about the eviction in advance.

"Father Dan hasn't been rightly at himself this while back," their mother had said, "and I wouldn't like him to be going down to the Master's at night.

He'll be more comfortable here with his own folk for a day or two anyway."

On the day after Father Dan's arrival, Bernard met old Nellie Sharkey on his way to the shop.

"What kind of form is His Reverence in?" she said.

"He's rightly," said Bernard.

Nellie shook her head backwards and forwards and made little noises with her tongue.

"God comfort the poor man!" she said. "Musha isn't it a pity of him? But he's luckier than some, thanks be to God. He can say Mass anyway, and that's a great blessing. When that poor priest in Drumbeg was put off the mission, he was left with nothing but his beads and his office."

Bernard said nothing. It was the first he had heard of Father Dan's troubles, but evidently they were common property.

The priest's presence did little to lighten the gloom of the house. He was moody and taciturn, and he seldom went further than the head of the street. He sat in the room for hours at a stretch, poring over his books, or paced the floor like a prisoner; and when he came up to the kitchen at night he was lost in his own bitter thoughts.

The neighbors who used to come "raking" at night dropped off one by one, and before a week was out only old Charlie Pat was left of the regulars. Charlie came because he couldn't do otherwise. The habit of years was so strong in him that he couldn't face for bed until he had had a spell at the Logues' fireside. He still came, but he no longer settled himself for a night's crack. He came early and he left early, and while he was there he was as edgy as a dog with fleas.

Father Dan never came up to the kitchen until

Charlie had gone. Then he would sit near the fire, looking down over his pipe at the play of the flames. He was a changed Father Dan. He spoke no more of Salamanca or Valladolid, or of the early frosts of the high Meseta, and the look in his eyes was a lost and lonely look.

After a little while he would rise and say, "It might be no harm to say the Rosary, Anthony. It's pushing on." And he would say the third decade himself, with a pitiful humility. It was as if he was admitting his degradation and savoring the full bitterness of it. Afterwards they would hear him pacing the room, and there would be a rim of light under his door until late in the night.

A week after Father Dan's arrival, news of Hughie came in a letter from Maggie Dunleavy the Brig, who was married to a policeman in Liverpool. Nora Logue read it slowly, forming the words with her lips. Then she wiped her eyes in the corner of her apron and passed it to her husband. Anthony took his glasses from the window and moved over to get the light from the half-door. When he had finished reading, he folded the letter back into its envelope and put it into his pocket. There was a blank look in his eyes.

Ellen, who was the youngest, began to sob.

"What's wrong, ma? What's wrong? Is Hughie dead? oh, is Hughie dead?"

Nora rose and put her arms about the child.

"Oh, a thaisge, what put that notion into your head! Don't vex yourself, child dear. There's nothing the matter with Hughie. Hughie's alive and well, and God will look after him."

Bernard heard the news that night from his father. Hughie had been in a public house brawl in Liverpool, and he had spent a fortnight in jail.

"He might have got a longer sentence," Maggie Dunleavy had written, "but Bill put in a word for him with the inspector and he got a good character in the court. I didn't want to worry you, God knows, so I didn't write before now, but Hughie is out again and he is knocking round with a crowd of drunken wasters. Bill tried to advise him for his own good, but it was no good. If Hughie keeps with these fellows he will get into more mischief. Some of you should come over, Bill says, and bring him home."

Father Dan made light of the whole business.

"A storm in a teacup," he said. "Any young fellow away from home and quick to raise his fists could easily get into a scrape like that. And many a better man has done a turn in jail and been none the worse for it."

"Aye," said Nora, "but bad company will be the ruination of him. Poor Hughie is easily led."

"Nothing has happened yet that can't be mended," said Father Dan. "But Maggie Dunleavy is right. A big city is no place for Hughie. He'll have to come home, and the sooner the better. Home is the only place for him."

Nora was red-eyed from weeping.

"But how can we get him home? Sure we don't know his address or a thing. We can't even write to him."

"Leave it to me!" said Father Dan. "I'll go over and bring him home—aye, if I have to drag him by the hair of the head. God knows I'm not much of an example to him, but I'll bring him home if it's the last thing I do."

Anthony Logue shook his head.

105 .

"No, Father Dan, it's no job for you. You're a priest, and it wouldn't be right that you'd be mixed up in a thing like this. If anyone goes for Hughie, it'll be me. I'm his father, and it's the poor hand I made of his rearing, but maybe it's not too late to talk sense into him. I'll leave for Liverpool the morra morn."

"You'll do no such thing, Anthony. You'll stay here with your wife and weans. You'd be lost in a big city. I'll go for Hughie. A priest can find out things more easily than a layman. People talk to him more readily. Besides, when a boy kicks over the traces his father is not always the best one to settle the harness on him again. In God's name, Anthony, I'll go to Liverpool, and I know that Hughie will listen to. me. There's no real badness in the gasur."

Anthony held out for a while, but Father Dan had his way in the end, and he went down to the room to pack the small black bag that was shaped like a long sausage roll. As usual, he made a great fuss of his packing, clawing through his possessions and shouting questions, looking for the toothbrush that he had packed already and wanting to know if anyone had seen his best stock. But he was in better form than he had been in for days, and when he came up to the kitchen again he was whistling tunelessly.

"Run down to Micky Anton, like a good boy," he said to Barney, "and tell him to be here in the morning in time to drive me up for the first boat."

He sat by the fire for a while then, but he was very fidgety, and soon he was on his feet again. He took a chair over to the loft and reached up for his fishing rod.

"It's a long time since you and I did a bit of fishing," he said to Bernard. "Get that old rod of yours and we'll try our luck in the Big Burn for a wee while."

There was a flood in the burn that evening. Two days of heavy rain had swollen its heavy feeders. Bernard and Father Dan stood for a minute at the end of the village and watched the opaque water surging smoothly under the single eye of the bridge. Lower down, where it flowed through a narrow ravine crossed by a small wooden bridge, the river was more turbulent; and lower still it had broadened into a great pool that encroached on the marshy lowlands where Davy Ann's cows got hungry feeding.

They crossed the bridge at the end of the village and kept to the moorland road until they came to Davy Ann's lane. Here they turned left and towards the sea, and after a hundred yards or so crossed a stone dyke and made their way down a small path at the edge of a field from which maincrop potatoes had been lifted a little earlier. It was heavy going. The wet grass tugged at their feet, and straggly briars reached for their faces. When they reached the river they scrambled along the bank until they came to the top of the pool, near the waterfall, where the brown water was strangely smooth out of the bubbly rush of the current.

Father Dan was panting a little.

"This will do rightly. We've come far enough. If there's a fish in the burn at all, it'll be here."

He took his rod out of its cloth case and began to fit the pieces together. Bernard's makeshift sally rod needed no grooming, and he had time to tumble a bru of grassy sod and collect some worms in a rusty box.

107 .

The burn was in noisy spate. Pieces of wood and uprooted bushes came down with the current, and there was a creaming of soiled froth bubbles where the water broadened out in the lee of the fall.

They fished in silence, spitting the worms on their hooks and dropping them into the brown water. There was no skill in this kind of fishing. It needed no strategy. When you felt a tug on the line you pulled in a mountainy trout and baited your hook again. The fish made poor fight of it. The biggest of them, placed lengthways on a man's hand, would not have gone far up his wrist.

Father Dan caught two trout, and he did not bait his hook a third time. He placed his rod upright against the slope of the bank, took out a round tobacco tin, and filled his pipe slowly. When he cupped his hands and held a match to the bowl, the flame lit up the strong muscles of his jaw, and his white hair made a thatch for his head.

He drew strongly on the pipe, tapping the tobacco home with an asbestos forefinger and making sucking noises. He might have been eating the tobacco instead of smoking it.

Bernard's line was still in the water, stretched out by the tug of the current. He had little interest in catching mountain trout, but he did not want to stop fishing until Father Dan had made it clear that he had had enough.

"What age are you now, son?"

"Seventeen past, Father."

The priest nodded his head.

"Seventeen. Aye. That's what I was thinking. But you're big enough for twenty. If you keep growing at this rate there's no knowing where you'll stop."

Father Dan puffed at his pipe. The clutch of his teeth on the curved stem gave a pout to his mouth, and the bowl of the pipe rested on his chin.

"You're a good lad. You have a head on your shoulders . . . I wish I could say as much for Hughie . . . But there's no badness in Hughie. He's just a wee bit foolish, and he's not the only one. And he'll get pardon sooner than some of us."

There was no smoothness in his speech. His words came in bursts, with puffs of smoke to speed them.

"Holy Orders makes priests of us, son, but it leaves us men."

Bernard said nothing. He looked at the slope of his line in the brown river and listened to the tumble of the waters. But he knew that the priest was staring straight in front of him and seeing nothing at all.

"A priest's life isn't an easy one. Sometimes people don't realise this. He has great privileges, but heavy burdens are laid on him. He is a man apart, and he can be lonely at times. . . . My trouble is the drink, lad, and God knows that's no secret now. The whole world knows it."

Bernard lifted in his line. He wound it slowly round the top of the rod and caught the hook in a loop of the cord. His hands were shaking, and there was a tightness in his throat.

"It's like a disease . . . I sometimes think that it *is* a disease. It's a craving in the blood. And it runs in the stock I come from. It follows us like a curse."

Bernard kept his eyes on the swollen river. The words he heard did not make full meaning for him. There was a time lag between sound and sense. He was to recall them afterwards many a time, for they were whorled indelibly in his mind, but just now he was numbed, and shocked, and full of pity.

A priest was a priest. He was as different from ordinary men as day from night. He had always thought of priests as men above sin and temptation, as men exalted, and sanctified, and changed forever.

"I'm off the mission now. Maybe for six months, maybe for a year. It all depends on the bishop—and on myself. The bishop is a good man, and a holy man. He gave me every chance. He gave me warnings enough, God help him. And it broke his heart to have to banish me."

A half-submerged trunk came down with the current. It lifted its nose clear of the water at the brink of the fall before it plunged down. It was like a bloated body.

"For the time being, I can do nothing but wait —that and fight this craving that at times seems almost as strong as life itself.

"I shouldn't be telling you all this. Or maybe I should. It mightn't do you any harm to know that priests are men like all the rest, and that they have their weaknesses and failings. Besides, it does me good to talk."

He paused for a little while then.

"And don't speak of this to anyone. Not even to your father and mother. They know the whole story, of course, but we don't speak about it. And silence can be a terrible kind of charity at times."

Father Dan took his rod asunder and began to slip the pieces into the cloth cover.

"Don't speak to anyone about it. Let it be a secret between us. But pray for me. And pray for Hughie too. Some of us need more prayers than others. Take your rod now and we'll be going."

He said nothing more until they had walked up

110 .

along the edge of the field again and crossed the stone dyke to the road.

"Tell me this, son," he said then. "You're on the brink of manhood now. Have you ever thought of what you're going to be?"

It was a strange question. Now that Hughie had left home, the whole thing was settled—at least until Barney could take over the work of the farm. Until then, Bernard would be working with horses, cutting turf and stacking it, thinning turnips and spraying potatoes. And there was no certainty that he would ever get away, for Barney might have notions of his own.

"I'll just work on the farm, I suppose."

"But when Hughie comes home? There won't be work for two young fellows on the farm."

"I don't think Hughie will ever come home, Father. Now that he has got his heels with him he'll be for staying."

Father Dan stopped for a second, and then walked on.

"He'll come home. Never you fear. I won't leave Liverpool without him."

"If he does," said Bernard, "I might go to Scotland. They say there's plenty of work to be had along the Clyde."

"You're young yet for Scotland. Don't do anything in a hurry. Many a one goes to Scotland and rues it."

"Or I might study for the police."

"You haven't any other plans in your head?"

"No," said Bernard.

There wasn't anything else. There couldn't be anything else. You stayed at home, or you went to Scotland or the States, or you joined the R.I.C.

"Ah, well," said Father Dan, "you have plenty of

time yet to make up your mind. Sometimes the solution comes suddenly and when you least expect it."

And he said no more until they reached the house.

Bernard's mind was still on what he had heard at the burn, and by comparison this roadside conversation seemed desultory and unimportant. But often during the months that followed the two seemed linked in some way. He could not trace the connection clearly at first, but gradually he came to see that Father Dan might have had a double purpose in bringing him fishing that evening.

Father Dan came up from the room a good hour earlier than usual that night. He seemed in much better humor, and he chatted with an animation that he had not shown for a long, long time. Later he fell into a reverie. His eyes, narrowed under their heavy brows, stared at the fire, and his teeth were clenched on his pipe.

He hadn't told a story for many a day, but he told one now, suddenly and without preamble.

"There was a poor widow who lived in Connemara during the penal times. She had one son, and he went to Salamanca for his priesting. It wasn't easy getting away in those days, and death was the penalty if you were caught. But the lad got a passage on a wine ship from Galway to Vigo, and found his way to Salamanca.

"The long years passed, and no word came from him. That wasn't surprising, considering the times that were in it. The long years passed, and the widow's hair grew whiter. She prayed every night that her son would come home a priest and give her his blessing before she died, but in the end she almost gave up hope. The lad might have been caught by a British frigate and hanged out of hand. He might have died fighting for France or Spain. Ten years was a long time, and anything might have happened to him.

"One wild wintry night, a stranger came to the widow's door. He was a tall, well-made man, and his heavy coat was soaked through.

" 'Could you give me food and shelter for the night?' he asked.

" 'Shelter I will give you willingly, stranger, and you are welcome to whatever food I have in the place. I have no meat, but I can give you oat cake and butter and fresh milk and as many eggs as you can eat.'

" 'A hungry man could ask nothing better,' said the stranger.

"He took off his wet cloak and stretched his legs to the fire, whilst the widow busied herself cooking eggs in a pot and laying the table. When the meal was ready he sat in to the table and started on the oat cake and eggs. He ate two eggs, and then two more. When he reached for the fifth the widow stared at him in wonder.

" 'I knew only one other man,' she said, 'who could eat five eggs at a sitting,' she said. 'My only son.'

" 'And where is he now?'

" 'God only knows,' said the widow. 'He sailed to Spain ten years ago, and I have been waiting for word of him ever since. If he is still living, he must have changed a lot in that time.'

"The stranger rose to his feet.

" 'He must have changed a lot indeed,' he said, 'since his own mother doesn't know him.'

" 'God be praised!' said the widow, taking her

113 .

son in her arms. 'He has answered my prayers and blessed my old age.'

"Then she knelt at his feet, and he blessed her in the name of the Father, and the Son, and the Holy Ghost."

A piece of turf crumbled in the fire, and the sound of the wind could be heard round the gable end of the house.

Father Dan rose and knocked the dottle from his pipe.

"It might be no harm if you began the Rosary, Anthony," he said. "I'll be having an early start in the morning."

9.

It was a raw, frosty morning when Father Dan climbed up on to Micky Anton's sidecar to begin his journey. He was wrapped in his Salamanca cloak, and he stood up to wind the rug round his middle and tuck it under him. The whole household saw him go, and they stood watching until the sidecar rose from the dip of the moorland road and began to climb Croc Ard. When it was three-quarters of the way up it disappeared as suddenly as if it had passed through a magic opening in the heart of the mountain, and been lost for ever, like the children of Hamlin.

After that, there was nothing to do but wait; to wait for night and dawn and gloaming; to say the Rosary, and milk the cows, and listen to the bubbling of the stirabout pot, and go out to the gable end of the house to watch for Jimmy the Post.

Father Dan wrote three times in ten days that seemed as long as ten months. Nora Logue opened the letters clumsily and eagerly, and craned into the window-light to read them. And when she had finished a letter she would put it into the neck of her dress, and sit down by the fire and say nothing at all. When Anthony came in—even when he was working in the fields he would find some excuse for coming back to the house about post time—she would hand him the letter in silence.

"Maybe we'll have news the morra," Anthony would say afterwards. "After all, Liverpool is a big city and it'll take time to search it. But you can trust Father Dan. We'll have news soon, never fear. Aye, maybe we'll get word the morro."

But there was no news the morra, or the morra's morra. There was no news of Hughie Logue, then or ever after. It was as if the earth had swallowed him up.

Father Dan spoke to priests and policemen, to lodging house keepers and dock laborers. He combed the city over and over. He visited hospital wards and billiard rooms and dance halls. He followed clues until they petered out. And in the end he lost heart and came back.

Jimmy the Post was an inquisitive body, but he had his code. He was thirsting for news of Hughie, but he was circumspect as well as oblique in his enquiries, and he never probed until his bag was empty. Each time he brought a letter to the Logues he turned away as if the secrecy of Her Majesty's mails extended even to postmarks, and it was not until he had done the rounds of Lurgabrack, and Meentagh, and the townlands along the shore, and so, in a sense, was no longer on duty, that he attempted to brief himself on the business of the countryside.

And even on his way back, he gave information before he asked for any. He talked about Larry Melia's new mare, or the fact that the spuds weren't keeping too well this year, or the progress of Constable Dooley's persistent courtship of Mary Donaghy the Brig. Then, just before he left, and with the air of one making a mannerly routine enquiry, he would say, "All going well with the boys, I hope?"

"Aye, thank God," Mrs. Logue would answer. "They're both doing rightly." But her eyes could not hide the cold truth.

Father Dan came back from Liverpool empty-handed. This was disappointment, but it was not heartbreak. The heartbreak came later. The weeks stretched into months, and the months lengthened into years. Hope was postponed from seed-sowing to harvest, and from Advent to lambing time. But the year never reached its turn for the woman who was always listening for a footfall, for the woman who had the same background to her thoughts whether she was saying her beads or knitting thick grey socks with colored heels and toes, or catching the hook of the griddle in her apron to lift it from the crane.

"If he had only written," she would say. "Losing him would be bad enough, God knows, but it's losing him the way I did that hurts. Not knowing where he is or how he is, or whether he's alive or dead. If he would only write once in a while it wouldn't matter, but he never puts pen to paper."

But she hadn't lost him. She never lost him. She spent her life waiting and hoping.

Anthony Logue took it hard too, but in his own

117 .

way. He kept his thoughts to himself, but the hurt had gone deep. He went to his grave ten years afterwards, but his wife hungered on for ten more, waiting for the letter that never came, listening for a footfall on the flags of the street, and hoping for a shadow across the half-door.

Father Dan stayed only a week in the Glen after his return from Liverpool. He went to stay with his brothers in Glasgow. In the Glen he was a silenced priest, and the wordless pity of the people only added to the burden it was meant to ease, but he could be anonymous in a big city. He stayed in the Glen only a week, and he was going almost from the moment he came.

In practical affairs, he was like a child. He couldn't tie a parcel properly, or remember to send his boots to the mend, or keep track of shirts and semmits. In the middle of his packing he would kneel beside the trunk with a book or a bundle of old letters in his hand and read for a solid hour. Packing was a torture to him. He would try to shoot home the clasps of his trunk by sitting on the lid, then he would raise the lid again to bruise in bulges of clothing, and finally he would postpone the operation and sit smoking at the kitchen fire.

This was not an ordinary departure. It was an evacuation; and the problem, as Father Dan saw it, defied solution. He wanted to bring with him everything that he had ever brought to the Glen, and to bring it on Micky Anton's sidecar. In the end, there was nothing for it but to choose this and reject that, and many of the books and papers had to be off-loaded. It was Bernard who finished his packing for him, and he did it by taking everything out and starting afresh, building from the bottom up like a man working at a stack of peats.

"I'll be back for them some time, if God spares me," said Father Dan, "and maybe sooner than you think. In the meantime you can keep an eye to them. They'll shorten the winter for you and give you something for the long nights."

"I'd like to have a talk with you before I go," he said after a little while. "We'll take a dander up the road for a while and get some fresh air into our lungs."

But he said very little, and it was only when they were almost back at the house again that he broke silence.

"I want you to pray for me, and I want you to pray for Hughie. If you put your mind to it you could manage a right wheen of prayers between now and Christmas . . . And do your best to make up to your mother for Hughie's going. She's a good woman, and he has given her heart a sore dunt . . . It would be little enough if he sent her a few lines once in a while . . . Be good to her while you're here, for I have a notion that you won't spend the rest of your days in the Glen."

Micky Anton scratched his head when he saw the pile of luggage that the priest had with him.

"Why the blazes didn't he bring a creel of turf and a few boxes of eggs when he was at it?" he said. "I doubt if the mare will ever make the turn at Croc Ard with all that stuff on her back."

Micky sat on one side of the car, with a suitcase for company, and a trunk as big as a sarcophagus went in the well. On the other side, Father Dan was barricaded with boxes and parcels, which were handed up to him or built about him. He had books and overflows of clothes, he had two currant scones, and a chicken, and bags of dulse and carrigeen moss.

"I'm in no danger of starvation for a fortnight at least," he said when they were ready to start. "And I'll take a run over to see you early in the New Year."

But he never came back, and he was dead before the blossoms came on the potatoes.

The Logues were sorry to see him go. He was their own kin, and the Glen had always been a second home to him. He brought life and color to it, and the breath of faraway places. During his last visit he had been gloomy and morose, but there was a reason for that. Besides, his black humors never lasted very long. They thawed before they had time to harden properly.

When he wrote at Christmas he sent a sovereign in a registered letter, though he had few sovereigns to spare at the time. He liked Glasgow, he said, but its fogs were hard on his chest and he hadn't been keeping too well. He wouldn't attempt the crossing during the hard weather, but as soon as the frosts went and the days began to lengthen properly he would take a run to the Glen.

He wrote again towards the end of February saying that he would have to postpone his visit for a while. He had a cough that he couldn't shake off, and he had spent a few days in bed off and on.

That was his last letter. News of his death came in May, and some cuttings from the Glasgow papers. His brother Colm wrote to say that "He got a wetting and it went to his lungs and he did no good after it." The weakness that had carried off so many of his family had overtaken him at last.

"It was a sad and lonely end for a priest," Nora Logue said. "But maybe not so lonely after all. He was as near to God and His blessed Mother in Glasgow as he would be anywhere else, and his bed is with the saints."

Father Dan was gone, and his weakness with him. He became a trimming to the Rosary in the house where he had dreamed of Salamanca.

Bernard prayed for him, as he had been bidden. He prayed for Father Dan and he prayed for Hughie. He bracketed the two intentions and made one intention of them. He prayed for Hughie and Father Dan. He spent his life praying for them.

10 .

December was more than half spent, and Bernard was feeling a lot better. He was feeling a lot better, but he was still on the broad of his back.

"When are you going to let me up?" he said to Sister Magdalena one Saturday morning. "Surely I'm well enough now to hobble out as far as the chapel! I'd like to be able to get to Sunday Mass at least. At this rate I'll be here till Easter."

Magdalena tucked in the clothes at the foot of the bed before she answered. "You get holy Communion every morning. When you're ready to get up, we'll let you up. And it is the doctors who will decide that."

"But what am I to do in the meantime?"

The blue eyes flashed at him.

"It wouldn't do you any harm to read your Missal."

"Aye, I suppose you're right, girl." Teaching her grandfather to suck eggs, she is, he said to himself, and aren't I the big, quiet soul not to answer her back. How could a man get through Advent properly without his Missal?

"Stir up our hearts, O Lord, and prepare the ways of Thine only-begotten Son . . . May we receive, O Lord, Thy mercy in the midst of Thy temple, that we may prepare with due honor for the approaching feast of our redemption . . . Populus Sion, ecce Dominus veniet ad salvandas gentes."

On the Sunday, he had a deluge of visitors. First Father Killian and Father Jerome, then the Prior and Father Stanislaus, and then Brother Paul, alone and inarticulate. After that came Johnny Mulligan and Jer Crowley, two of the Sodality prefects, with a bag of grapes apiece.

You could have too many visitors, Bernard was thinking. You tired yourself pitying them. The man in the bed had the advantage. He was at the wicket, the others had to do the bowling. And Mulligan and Crowley, God help them, were bad bowlers. They fiddled with their hats and talked about the weather, and they were obviously determined, in spite of their lack of ammunition, to stay for a respectable length of time.

They had hardly gone when big Lar Kerrigan from the fruit market put his head round the door and looked from bed to bed.

"How the divil are you, Brother?"

He shook hands as enthusiastically as a councillor at election time, threw his hat on the bed, and sat down heavily. He was a mountain of a man, with an enormous head and hanging jowls. There were double wads of fat under his chin, and his stomach had slipped from its moorings.

"It was only yesterday I heard you were sick." Lar always spoke like a man with a heavy cold. "Sure a man could be dead and buried these days without anyone hearing about it—except the undertaker, of course."

This was a palpable slip, and he retrieved it hurriedly.

"Though it's yourself looks like a man who won't be bothering the undertaker for a long time to come."

It was a ploy that Bernard was well used to by now, and he let it pass.

"How are you keeping yourself, Lar?"

"Gameball, thank God."

Lar was a carrier. He had a fleet of five horse-drawn "yokes," and two ton lorries. He had driven a lorry himself once, but that was long ago. In the meantime he had prospered and run to flesh.

"How are things in the markets, Lar?"

"Up and down, Brother. Up and down. Savoys are a desperate price. Anyone growing cabbage these days must be making a fortune."

"Plenty of apples, I suppose?"

"Lashings. Cookers and eaters. The market is full of them. And the Christmas trees are beginning to come in."

Bernard was thinking of his own apples. The eaters were all gone, but he still had a few Bramley cookers left. And he was thinking too of his trees. He felt lonely without them. Even in winter he was fond of taking an odd look at them, gnarled and unlovely as they were then. You could almost hear them breathing in their sleep. And they wakened long before they showed any signs of wakening. When the days lengthened, there would be a great stir in the roots, and the first touch of mild weather would see them budding.

"You won't feel it now till Christmas," said Lar when he rose to go. "It beats all how the time passes."

"It passes slowly enough here, Lar."

The big man considered this gravely, and nodded his great head.

"I suppose it does, Brother. I hadn't thought of that. But sure it won't be for long. You'll be out of this long before Christmas with the help of God. And all the lads is terrible sorry that you're laid up. Larboy, and Joeboy, and Raffler McGurk and all. Everyone of them was asking for you."

He was glad to see Lar, but he was glad too to see him go. He had had enough visitors for one day. His strength seemed to have ebbed since the morning, and his spirits had ebbed with it. He felt depressed and irritable and very, very tired.

Father Denbigh, the chaplain, was the last of his visitors. He liked Father Denbigh. He was a good talker, and he was as full of stories as an egg is full of meat. He could be a tonic at times, but he could be a trial too. You had to be in your health to cope with him.

He was a tall, good-looking priest, still on the right side of forty but balding before his time; relaxed, jovial, and bursting with energy. He passed through the wards every morning, preceded by an altar boy with bell and candle. He was reverent, vested, and purposeful then. He was a

125 .

priest, and he had God in his fist. In the afternoons, it was different. The other visitors brought grapes and chrysanthemums. Father Denbigh brought stories. He would tell stories till the cows came home.

Bernard remembered that evening. There was a ringing in his ears, and he could hear the thumping of his heart. Father Denbigh's voice rang in his head like a lighthouse bell.

The stories went on and on: the endless stories of a "gas character" who had been in Blackrock and Clonliffe with him. Never did a tap of work in his life but walked through all his exams. Did his doctorate in theology in Rome afterwards. The cheek of old Nick he had. When he was in Blackrock the Latin professor sent him up to the President for giving cheek in class. When he came back the professor asked him how he had got on. "Fair enough," says your man. "I had him by the throat, but he got away."

He was a gas character right enough. But Bernard was in no fettle for gas characters.

After every story, and sometimes in the middle of one, Father Denbigh would swing round to make sure that the rest of the class were attending. Patterson, who was well on the mend now, had his own way of laughing—his face creased, and his eyes glittered, but he made no sound. The Cavan farmer made no more response than a Chinese idol, and yet managed to convey that he disapproved of the whole business. The young civil servant who was in Briody's bed kept his elbows on his stitches.

Briody had gone home now, and his absence had its debit and credit sides as far as Father Denbigh was concerned. It meant that his audience was less enthusiastic. On the other hand, now he had the floor to himself. Briody had been generous with his laughter, but at any minute he might come up with a story of his own.

Bernard remembered that evening. Father Denbigh was very near and very far. His voice strengthened and ebbed by turns. His stories had no end.

Father Denbigh was back again in the early hours: deft, reverent, purposeful. But in the meantime much had happened.

Looking back on it afterwards, Bernard wondered if the whole thing had been a dream, or if his panic and despair had been merely the prelude to what followed, and his mental turmoil a reflex of things physical. But at the time it was like the shadow of the judgment. He was in a great emptiness where there was nothing but the self. And the self did not suffice. It was part of the emptiness about it. It was shrivelled and full of rottenness.

He saw his life dwindled to a small miserly accounting. There was nothing heroic in it, nothing worth recording. It was empty even of the big sins that bring men nearer to God. There had been no white heat of charity in him, no trampling of self, no conquest. He had been neither hot nor cold. He had given with one hand and held back with the other. He was the shadow of a religious. He had lived in a monastery, but he had been no more than a lodger there, paying his tally of prayers and service, keeping the rules, giving no bother. He had lived in a monastery, but his heart had been outside. The things he had loved were earthly things: places and people, colors and sounds, the pageant of life.

The account balanced, but there was no surplus.

And it balanced only because of the tiny totals on each side. It was a reconciling of infinitesimal things.

On his first night in the hospital, the thought of death had not frightened him. It had seemed as natural and as peaceful as the tolling of the Angelus bell. It would be welcome whenever God willed it. But now the thought of death chilled him to the marrow. If he went now he would be going with empty hands, with nothing to show for his stewardship, with no increase, no burgeoning, no shine of use on his talents.

He had peeled potatoes, and risen in the grey dawn, and kept silence, and tended his apple trees, and hacked weeds from between the stones of the garden path. He had obeyed his superiors, and begged shillings from door to door, and put flowers in vases, and snuffed out guttering candles. But all these tiny nothings had been sterile and profitless, because there had been no emptying of self, no surrender, no cumulative capitulation. He had not decreased as he should have decreased, and now he had nothing to lean on but God's mercy.

When he tried to pray, his words were as cold as his heart and they seemed to go no further than his lips. And then he seemed not to be praying but listening. Everyone since time began has had to lean on My mercy: Francis and Teresa, Moses and David, Sam Beckford and the Flapper Mulligan; the good and the bad, the tepid and the lukewarm, the saint and the sinner . . . Anything you have to confess is blacker than your confessing of it, and I alone can see sins in their proper size . . . But I thought you worth the making, and you were always in My mind. You were always in My mind as if you were the only thing of My making . . . I am your advocate as well as your judge. I bought you back at a great price, and I shall not let you go easily.

Afterwards he felt ashamed, not so much of his need of comfort as of the manner of his comforting. The words had come too glibly. He was giving himself airs and simulating a dark night of the soul. But at the time he felt comforted and reassured; and then, suddenly, very cold. It was as if all warmth had begun to ebb from him. It was life fluttering like a candle flame in the wind. It was the knocking of an importunate visitor.

He was ready and braced when the pain struck. It reefed his body in pulsating waves. It came in lightning flashes of white agony, until it could no longer be borne.

He was conscious for his anointing. The pain still came in rhythmic stabs, but its force was spent and its venom gone. He felt the touch of the holy oils on his eyelids and nostrils and open mouth, on his hands and feet.

Book and bell, candle and blessing. The battle was joined. The light and the darkness. This was the sacrament that Christ had made to match the need for it, to seize and brand a soul at the end, to mark it and number it, to strengthen and comfort, to summon the saints and banish the demons.

In a few moments, Father Denbigh would be back to size; he would strike matches, and bite at a cigarette, and back his car into the drive, and take off his stock, and drape his trousers over the back of a chair. But for the time being he was the King's man. He could brief Peter and Paul and chide Beelzebub. He could call on the Lord to deliver His servant, as He had delivered Lot from the brimstone, and Moses from Pharaoh, and Daniel from the lion, and the three children from the fiery furnace, and Susanna from her accusers, and David from Goliath, and Saul from prison. Nothing could withstand him; not principalities or powers, not things over the earth or on it or under it. His writ ran. He was acting for and on behalf of. He spoke with Christ's words and anointed with Christ's hands, and the angels were round his head.

11 .

Bernard awoke from a drugged sleep, and wondered at his freedom from pain. He tested his arms and legs. There was no rebellion in them. They moved as they had always moved.

A nurse appeared round the screen.

"You've had a fine sleep."

She wiped his face and hands with a damp towel, and he realized that he had been sticky with sweat.

"I'd like some tea, nurse."

"Certainly. I'll get it for you now."

"And toast."

Little things mattered again. Once the body was cleansed of fright and pain it wanted its egg boiled hard or its tea fine and strong or the sheet tucked in at the bottom.

Father Denbigh came in as he was finishing his

tea and toast. He slid between the screens and looked down at him. He was cheerful, smiling, matter-of-fact; looking as he looked at Senior Cup matches at Lansdowne Road, or at weekly whist drives, or at bring-and-buy sales. He was no longer acting for and on behalf of. His glory had abated. He was Jimmy Denbigh in a stock and round collar.

"Feeling better?"

"Yes, thank God." Bernard nodded.

Father Denbigh sat down and lit a cigarette. "You gave us a hell of a fright last night."

It was nothing to the fright I gave myself, Bernard was thinking.

"But there's not a bother on you now. You're a bit of a fraud, Bernard. You're grand again."

"Grand."

He could have made a song of that. He could have soldered it on to a Te Deum. Having no pain, he had everything. He felt good enough to stake up chrysanthemums, or fuel the cooker, or give bowls of soup to poor men, or play draughts with old Brother Joachim, who couldn't play for skins but who got so cranky if anyone beat him twice in succession that he had to be allowed to win every other game for the love of the brethren.

Bernard felt well, but he had no illusions. His anointing had solaced body and soul, but it had not mended or sutured. It had not exorcised physical facts. He might have imagined some things the night before, but he had not conjured up a seizure. There was no point in dodging the truth, and the truth stared him in the face. He had been as far as the brink and back again, and not for the first time.

He was better now, but it was only a respite at best. Since Capel Street Bridge he had been living on borrowed time. And yet he did not believe this—not fully. You played at being heroic and at facing facts, but you still hoped. Every easeful breath you drew was a promise.

There were easier ways of dying. A man could die in his sleep, or his breathing could quieten slowly until it stopped imperceptibly—he had seen men die like that. But there were harder ways, too, like being flayed alive. Or you might be crucified— the way the Reds had crucified the Canons of Toledo. A thought like that put fear into your very marrow. It shrivelled up the heart in you. But God picked His men. He matched the man and the manner of his going. He picked the hard men for the hard road.

Father Denbigh was quiet that afternoon. He pulled at his cigarette and said less than usual. He had no stories, no gales of laughter. Father Denbigh was quiet, and the ward was holding its breath. You could feel the tension. Patterson no longer read out paragraphs from the newspaper, and the civil servant had silenced his wireless.

Sister Magdalena came in, and Father Denbigh rose to his feet. They were like characters in a play, coming and going. The screens cut off the whole world.

Magdalena smoothed the coverlet and smiled at Father Denbigh. She was telling him in her own way that he had been there long enough and that he mustn't tire the patient.

"He's grand, Father. What he needs now is rest and quietness. . . . You should try to get a little sleep, Brother. It will do you good."

133 .

Father Denbigh stubbed his cigarette on the bed-side ashtray.

"Watch yourself, Bernard. I'll be seeing you."

He was under constant surveillance. Magdalena came and went on simulated errands. The house surgeon used his stethescope every couple of hours. Bernard was back in the leading part again. He was the number one exhibit.

The house surgeon said little or nothing. He fobbed off questions with smiles. He had no gift of words, but he knew his etiquette. Bernard was Mr. Williamson's patient, and a young doctor had to be circumspect. He did not want to be queried.

Williamson himself had been in in the morning. He was a tall, middle-aged man; grey-haired, hand-some, and beautifully groomed. He looked the part, and he might have been acting it. You might have placed him as a senator or a diplomat, but your first guess would have been Fitzwilliam Street or Merrion Square.

Mr. Williamson came back in the afternoon, which was unusual, for he was one of the Big Men, and he usually spaced his visits. And he did not content himself with heartiness and a snap inspection. He produced his stethescope like a conjuror and listened carefully to its story. He studied the charts, and the patient. He was very thorough, and very serious, and very silent.

Bernard quizzed him for the fun of it.

"How long do you give me, doctor? A week?"

Mr. Williamson played with his stethescope.

"Nonsense, Brother. You'll probably die of old age."

"At that rate, I haven't much further to go.

But tell me, doctor, what's the matter with me, and what happened to me last night?"

But the medical association was giving nothing away. It polished its spectacles and spoke of a "turn." It did not want to exaggerate, but it was only fair to say that the patient was not quite out of the wood yet. He had a heart condition that needed careful watching. They would have to keep an eye on him for a day or two.

Bernard did not pursue the point. Something was bound to go wrong sooner or later, and whether it was the lungs or kidneys or blood cells did not signify. When you were pushing on in years you could be certain that some part of the mechanism was nearing its breaking point. His own trouble was in the heart or its conduits—needle-thick or pencil-thick. The arteries panted in and out with the tide of the blood until the elasticity went out of them and they became lined with fur like an old kettle. Then, if a clot lodged in a sluice-gate, the whole pumping system shuddered into silence.

He knew very little about the business, and it might have been better, he thought, if he had known less. There was no use in thinking, or worrying, or hoping. The manner of your going was God's secret, and the wise thing was to leave it to Him, and ask Him to make it as light as He could manage.

Mr. Williamson came back in the morning and took more soundings.

"We're going to move you," he said. He might have been giving notice of an excursion, a legacy, or a promotion.

"Move me?"

"Oh, not very far."

"Are you going to operate?"

The big man shot this one down. "Oh, no. Nothing like that. You're not an operation case. What you need is rest and quiet, and you'd be better in a room by yourself."

Bernard smiled wryly. "I could have a room to myself in the monastery if you would let me go back."

"All in good time, Brother. All in good time. But for the present you're better in places where fellows like me can have a peep at you now and again . . . And we want to cut down on visitors for a little while."

"I see," said Bernard.

"This is just a temporary measure, of course. You'll be as right as rain again soon, please God. In the meantime you must leave things to us. And don't worry. Rest and quiet are what you need most. That's why we're moving you to a single room."

It sounded well, but it didn't make sense. No one could prescribe rest for you. Quietness was a thing of the mind; and the mind conjured up its own excitements. You could be relaxed listening to Father Denbigh, and agitated in solitary confinement.

He was moved upstairs that evening, with the complete removal crew in attendance: two nuns, a nurse, and Michael, the houseboy. They slid him onto a trolley as deftly as Brother Paul would slide a fried egg on a plate. They covered him with blankets and trundled him off. The Cavan farmer turned a cold dead eye towards him as he was

136 .

moved out and waved a hand lugubriously in sa-
lute.

The trolley moved noiselessly up the light blue
corridor, past doors with numbers on them, and
statued niches, and flowery window sills. Michael
and one of the nuns pushed; the other nun and the
nurse kept a hand on the blankets. They made him
think of dockers on the quay overstaffing a truck
and making up the statutory crew.

Michael came into the lift with him, and they
were carried upward with a soft whirring sound.
When the lift stopped, the trellis door clicked
open and he was wheeled along another corridor
that was the dead spit of the one below, and round a
corner where the walls had rounded edges.

The trolley docked at the bedside in a small
aseptic room, and he was slipped between the sheets
as if some overhead magnet had neutralized his
mass and bulk. The two nuns tucked him in, and
attacked the pillows with the irritating vigor of a
waiter brushing imaginary crumbs from a spot-
less table. They stowed his duds in the locker,
adjusted the window-blind, and spaced his hot-
water bottles.

"Now," said Sister Magdalena, "you're nice and
comfortable. There's nothing more you want?"

"Nothing," said Bernard. "You wouldn't have a
quid of tobacco about you, I suppose?"

"Try and get some sleep," said Sister Magdalena.
"Now you can have all the quietness you want."

"I could do with less," said Bernard.

When they had gone, he looked about him. On
the wall opposite there was a picture of the Sacred
Heart, and he knew that there was a crucifix over
his head. The window was on his left. Unlike the
window in the ward downstairs, it was made of

137 .

clear sheet glass. There was no muffing, so that he could look out at the green backcloth of the hills, with a sugar-dusting of snow on their high ridges, and at the spires and chimney of the city. But except in the distance it was a truncated city. It had been sliced off at roof-level.

It was quiet in the upper room. Downstairs, even when the screens were round his bed, he had had a feeling of companionship and was one of a community. Now he was cut off and alone; and yet not alone, for his thoughts had come with him. The furniture of his mind lay undisturbed under the dust-sheets of the years.

12.

Tom Logue came back to the Glen and to the house that had reared him, and came back so fully that he might never have left. His six years in Glasgow had left no mark on his speech, habits, or outlook. He came back to the Glen to wear heavy boots with thong laces, thick woolen socks, and homespun trousers. He cleaned the byre and foddered the grey mare. He ploughed and harrowed, he sowed and reaped. He cut turf on the mountain with an angled slean. He shaved in the kitchen on Saturday nights, and on Sundays he leaned against the stone dyke with the other men and then went into the church to kneel on his cap and dangle his beads.

He was a Glensman, and he was home again. He began where he had left off.

He was still on the right side of thirty, but there

were smudges of grey in his dark hair. The marks of suffering were on his thin, sensitive face, and there was a great loneliness in his eyes. Glasgow was a chapter in his life, and it was closed for ever. His wife and child were in the quiet earth, and he had come back to the place he knew, to the one place where there was healing for his hurt.

By Glen standards, he had married young, for the Glen men—both at home and abroad, and for the same reason—seldom married until they were long in the tooth. At home, they had to wait until the old folk were dead or doddering before they could bring home a wife or marry into a farm; and if they went to Glasgow or Philadelphia, they had to pay off an old debt and help to rear their brothers and sisters before they could save enough money to start a family and build a home of their own.

Tom Logue had sent home hard-earned money in his time, but he had cut free earlier than most. He had married a Fanad girl who was at domestic service in Maryhill, but she died in childbirth a year later, and her son barely survived his baptism. A month afterward, Tom was back in the Glen.

Work was the saving of him, and he turned to it as another man might turn to whiskey. He started work a full hour before the rest of the Glen, and he kept at it as long as there was a bit of light. He was fighting back in his own way.

The evenings were hardest on him. He would sit on a square, stiff-backed kitchen chair, or on the settle along the far wall, far from the glow of the fire. He smoked one fill of the pipe every night, paring the thick plug into his fist with a blackened knife, and taking his time about the filling. When the pipe was finished he tucked his hands under his elbows and wrapped himself in silence. His thoughts were far away, and no one queried them.

After a few weeks he would join sparingly and listlessly in the talk about rents and prices, deaths and marriages, and the weather prospects for Derryleigh Regatta. But it was a long long time before he could bring himself to talk about Clydeside, and when he did his mother's heart lifted. He was her first-born, and she had fussed over him unobtrusively ever since his homecoming. Now she knew that the fire of life was beginning to kindle slowly in him again, and that scars were forming on the wounds in his memory.

He never spoke about his wife or child, for the reticence of the Glen was strong in him. He spoke about the glow of the furnaces along the Clyde, and the crowds in Sauciehall Street. He had a good eye and a way of stringing words together, and when you listened to him you see the workers streaming out of the shipyards and hear men talking in quayside pubs about Glasgow Celtic and the fabulous Jimmy Quinn.

But there was no nostalgia in his talk, no regrets, no golden memories. He was no Father Dan remembering Salamanca. He had finished with the gantries and the clang of the hammers, with music halls and naptha flares and a navvy's wage packet. He had made his choice freely. The city had broken him, and he had come home to the fields that his fathers had made, to plow and harness and the drag of the cold soil. He would live and die in the Glen. He would be buried with his kinsmen in the crowded churchyard at Killard, where the salt tide came up to the roots of ancient trees, and ivy grew on mouldering walls, and every thrust of the spade disturbed old bones.

141 .

He spoke about the crowds and the busy shops and the blinding fogs that crept up from the Clyde and thickened until you could scarcely see your hand in front of your face, but he did more than paint a picture of Glasgow and the life he had known there. He put the picture in its historical setting. He linked it with the past and the future. He saw it as a chapter in the story of his race.

The descendants of the Scots settlers were thick in the province of Ulster. They were snugly settled in the rich river valleys, and they had every pocket of good land from Fair Head to Lifford. But now there was a great concourse of northern Irish in Glasgow and the mining towns about it. The grandsons of the dispossessed were seeping into the very heart of Scotland.

And they were not wholly exiles. Their English speech was strongly tinged with Scots, and the traditions that were rooted in them had once been shared by Argyll and Annagry. Many of them too were native Irish-speakers, and so, in spite of John Knox and the Covenanters, the Gaelic-speaking Highlanders were their kinsmen. They could speak to one another with a fair measure of understanding in a tongue that was once common to both sides of the Sea of Moyle and that had christened every lough and mountain north of the Rift Valley. It sounded barbarous to the Lowlanders, but it was a link of race and blood. The Gaelic of Barra and the Hebrides was of the same royal line as the Gaelic of Cruit and Gweedore.

The immigrants were despised for their poverty and their allegiance to Rome, but they bided their time. The Clydeside Irish were as thrifty as the Scots about them. They were hard-working and all-enduring. Hardship was no "neweens" to them, and sore toil was their birthright. They took the work that came their way. They sweated and wrought in the foundries, and crowded through the shipyard gates on frosty mornings; they spat on pick-handles and dug into the yellow topsoil to make drains and sewers and foundations; they washed glasses in public houses, and carried sides of beef in abattoirs, and opened little shops that blossomed into bigger shops. They lived in tenements and crowded "closes." Like the Jews, they were all-enduring. But their eyes were on the future. They saved their pennies, and educated their children, and built schools and churches. They were loyal to the way of life that they had brought with them from across the sea.

And in time they were accepted and integrated. They became a part of the prosperity that they helped to build, and they acquired a new loyalty to the land of their adoption. They outgrew the tradition of the despised "tattie-hokers" who had come in hunger to dig Scotland's harvest. The first immigrants were navvies and hod carriers, but their children and their children's children were free of sweat and hardship and were not indentured to knee-banded corduroy.

Tom had seen the beginnings of this movement, and if things had gone differently he might have been a part of it. But when he came home, he came home for good. He had thrown the dice, and he was prepared to abide the turn of the wheel.

In one way, Tom's homecoming eased things in the Glen. He had brought sixty pounds back with him—made up of his savings and the sale of his few sticks of furniture—and it all went into the household purse. The Logues had never had much money, apart from the hoarded sovereigns that covered the rent and strong shoes for the winter. Now, thanks to Tom, there was a nest egg in the cupboard, and they could sleep more easily. They were secure against dark and unforeseen tragedies —like the loss of a beast, or a wet harvest, or bad luck with the mountain sheep. They had something put by against the day of the sore leg.

Tom, moreover, had come home with a new skill. As a laboring jack-of-all-trades in the shipyard he had worked with welders and masons and joiners, and he had picked up a smattering of many crafts. He could mix mortar and build walls, he could angle rafters and lay slates, and he had some skill with a saw. Little by little he began to put a better shape on the farm outbuildings. He proved himself by knocking down the sagging end wall of the byre and rebuilding it straight as a lance, and then he started to work odd days with Corny Green, the local mason, when the farm work was slack.

This new venture brought in little money, for Corny couldn't afford to pay very much. Most of his contracts were for staunching and repair work rather than for building proper, and it was only once in a while that he got the chance of putting up a new house for some family that had got an American legacy. But a pound or two meant a lot in the Glen, where the rattle of sovereigns in a goose-necked purse was the sign of a man of substance, and the extra money that Tom earned made a big difference in the Logues' finances.

And he worked for the household, not for himself. He kept a few shillings for tobacco, but the rest was handed up. If he stayed, the place would be his some day; if he went, he would leave his people with a better way on them. But it soon became clear that he intended to stay, and, although he was still a young man, that he had no notion of marrying again. He had lost one woman, and he never looked at another.

His homecoming had eased one problem, but it had raised another. There were three grown men in the house by the Burn now, and another who was stretching daily, and this was a problem that suggested its own solution. In the Glen a man might keep one of his sons at home to take the burden of the heavy work and inherit the holding eventually, but this was as much as the local economy allowed. One son stayed at home. The others were a surplus for export.

Anthony Logue was still in the early sixties, but his rheumatism had slowed him down and he was not as supple as he used to be. He still decided the schedules for seed-sowing and harrowing, for thinning and spraying and harvesting, but for almost ten years he had delegated the harder work of the farm to those who were more fitted to do it: to Hughie, when Tom went to Scotland; to Bernard, when Hughie left; and now to Tom again. Bernard and Barney did their share, but Tom was in the saddle. There was no appointing, no formal change of status. Tom was the first-born, and that was that.

To the mind of the Glen, Bernard was the gainer by this new arrangement. Before, he had been spancelled and tied; now he was free. There was nothing to keep him at home. He could be off as soon as he had scraped up the passage money for his going. He could go to Derry, and sail to Glasgow for a few shillings, or to Boston or New York for a few pounds.

Those who were free to go were envied; those who stayed, stayed perforce. To stay was to be apprenticed forever to clabar and slavery, to heavy boots and a light purse, to the long dark nights, and the cold fields, to the smell of the byre and the roughness of woolen shirts. When you stayed, you were a lodger in your father's house, an unpaid laborer on his farm. You worked for your keep, and the chapel pennies, and a couple of shillings on Regatta Day.

Courtship there might be, but it was often a heartbreak and a mockery and a frustration, and it was almost always long postdated. Marriage had to be postponed until death left a vacant seat or a vacant bed, or until the old people were doting and querulous; and a man might be rising fifty before he could bring home a woman of his own. And there was no such thing as building a home. The bride came into a home that was of someone else's making. She might not be mistress of it for years, and in the meantime she had to listen to the grumblings of the old woman in the chimney-seat and learn the truth that no house is big enough to hold two women. She milked cows, and baked bread, and boiled potatoes, and washed heavy shirts, and mixed hen food in tin pandies, and rose soon after childbirth to pad about an earthen floor.

All this might be bearable enough, and it often added up to happiness, but to young people it was a prospect that chilled. It seemed like a blind and pitiful mortgaging of youth and hope, for the young will do anything but wait, and for them the only desirable thing is the thing that is done here and now.

It was better to get away, and to go young. You might have to slave with pick and shovel, but you would at least have money in your purse, and there was always the chance of bettering yourself. Tom Lynch of Meentagh, who was credited with having worn out three First Books and with never passing the Third, had a saloon in Brooklyn, and Ned Big Hughie of Lurgameelon had three butter and egg shops in Glasgow. Crossing the sea was always a gamble, but if things turned your way you might finish up as well as John Boyle the Brig, who was a contractor in Hartford, Connecticut, and had seventy men working for him. And at the worst you would have a better way on you than the ones at home. You could marry a wife when the fit was on you and not have to wait until you were long in the tooth and your head was thatched with gray and the glory was gone from your stride and bearing.

You might have to sweat in the glare of the furnaces or the smell of the stockyards, but you would have a corner of your own to go home to at night. And you wouldn't leave hardship as a legacy to your children; they would have meat every day, and chances that they would never have at home.

In the Glen, the talk of the young people was always about faraway places. They talked about Wishaw and Motherwell, Airdrie and Coatbridge; Chicago, Illinois, and Cleveland, Ohio. Within limits, their knowledge of geography was detailed and particular. Their texts were letters with foreign postmarks, and they knew to a dollar or two what a ganger could earn in a day on the Chesapeake and Ohio Railroad.

Tom's homecoming gave Bernard a visa that he could use at any time. He was free to go when the notion took him, and he knew that he would leave the Glen sooner or later. But for the time being there was no hurry on him. Looking back now, he could not decide what it was that made him defer his going, but he knew that the look in his mother's eyes had a part in it. She never talked to him about it, but he knew that she wanted to hold him for a while. She was still thinking of Hughie, and it was a comfort to her to have the rest of her menfolk about her.

He knew too that the old people of the Glen did not cede their children without heartbreak. He had seen too many "convoys" in his time to have any illusions on this point. The emigrants usually left in groups, and the "convoy" was the farewell party held on the eve of their departure. Chickens would be killed, and strong tea brewed, and the poteen flowed freely. It was a night of feasting and story telling, and the fun went on until morning; but it was also a night of sorrow, and it was with cause that people often spoke of convoys as "American wakes."

The young folk were light-hearted enough, but the old people sat in silence until the poteen loosened their tongues and then they broke out into wild laments. They knew that when their children crossed the sea they were usually lost to them forever, and they looked into futures that held nothing but loneliness and the creaking of old bones. This was the real heartbreak of the Glen —where life could be happy enough at times—and the most bitter and most lasting curse of the Plantations: that a house could be full of weans and lose them one by one, that a child was a child only till he was ready for the road, and that every family was building up to a scattering.

148 .

13.

It was Bernard's third evening in the upper room. He was making headway, he felt, though he did not trust his feelings too much. The doctors said they were pleased with his progress, but he was not too sure of the doctors either. All he knew for sure was that he had had no recurrence of pain, that he was eating well, and that if feeling were any guide he was fit for discharge.

When he turned his head on the pillow he could see a frieze of roofs and spires, and the shadowy bulk of the hills. The winter dusk came on early, and when the darkness strengthened he looked down on two sudden rows of street lights that pared to an arrowhead beneath the red glow over the heart of the city.

The lights of Dublin had changed a lot in his

time. He remembered when there had been gas lamps in the streets: one-legged lamps with two short bars on which little girls hung ropes for swinging. The gas lamps burned with a tremulous white flame, and there was a blueness at the base of the mantle like shaving shadow on a man's chin. At twilight, the uniformed lamplighter scurried along like a man who despaired of finishing his work in time, pushed his red-nosed rod through a slot in the bottom of the lamp, and hurried off before the blue flame flowered into full incandescence.

After that came white electric lights. But white light was old-fashioned nowadays. The experts had found that it cast shadows, or was too hard on the eyes, or became bleary when mist was about, and now the street lights were ghostly green or watery yellow. They made faces look bilious, but the knowing ones said that they cast fewer shadows. For that matter, there was scarcely any need now for public lighting. The city was full of blazing, apocalyptic signs; red arrows pointed to select lounges, petrol pumps were indicated by metal men with luminous heads; and fried-fish parlors, cinemas, and hire-purchase shops turned night into day.

And the lights spread over the whole world. Neon was the new international language. There was no more darkness except in the hearts of men.

Over the lights were the roofs, and under the roofs were the people: old and young, black and white, wise and foolish; each of them going about his own business and keeping his own secrets, and all of them making up the multitudinous clamor of the world. And seeing it all, permitting it all, suffering it and loving it eternally, was the Man Above. Without Him, the earth and the firmament

150 .

above and about it was a thought to crush the poor shell of the mind. With Him, it had meaning and purpose. He held all things in the hollow of His hand.

Sister Augustine came in with his nightcap of hot milk and biscuits, and a little white tablet that would do something to him while he slept. You took these potions on trust, knowing nothing, believing everything. It was modern magic.

When Augustine went off duty, Nurse Kelleher would take over. She would come in a few times during the night on routine checks, to make sure that you were still breathing. If you wanted some special service, you pressed the bell over the bed —provided of course that you were able to reach it in time and set a little red light blinking in the office across the corridor. But there was no guarantee that you could reach the bell in time, and then, when she came next she would find you staring at the ceiling and not seeing even the darkness.

"Well, and how are we tonight?" said Sister Augustine.

This was the medical "we," the psychological "we," the "we" hearty and reassuring. It made illness a communal affair.

Bernard swallowed his pill with a chaser of milk.

"Fair enough, ma'am. Fair enough."

He liked Sister Augustine. She was tall and stout; a motherly woman with warm brown eyes and a placid face.

"I was looking out at the lights."

"You should go to sleep. I'll draw the blinds."

He looked up at her, and ran a finger round the rim of his tumbler.

151 .

"Leave them be, woman dear. What harm are they doing me? If I want to go to sleep the lights won't stop me, and if I'm lying awake they're good company."

"You're sure they don't keep you from sleeping?"

"Divil a fear. How are things in the hospital? Comings and goings, I suppose."

"This is always a slack time. We only get emergency cases now, for anyone who can puts off coming to hospital until the New Year, and those that are here are anxious to get home for Christmas."

He began to nibble a biscuit. "It's something I never did."

"What?"

"Go home for Christmas. When I left home I left for good. Did you ever go home for Christmas?"

"Not since I entered, of course. But I used to, years ago, when I was at a boarding school. It was great. We were always awake at the dawn."

"You lived in the country?"

"Yes. In Kilkenny, near Piltown."

"Where the apples come from?"

"Where the good apples come from."

He set down his glass and folded his arms.

"In Donegal, where I was reared, there were very few apples, and the few there were were sour and crabbed. The salt sea air scorched the trees, and the moss grew on the trunks."

He would have liked to tell her then of the four apple trees in the monastery garden. They were sleeping now, and looking as if they would never wake. But they would foam and blossom in the spring, and with God's help he would be there to see them. But Augustine was poised for flight. The nuns talked, but never for the sake of talking. They had work to do, and they lived to a strict schedule.

"Good night, Brother. You should turn off the light and go to sleep."

"In a little while, Sister. In a little while. Good night to you now. And God bless you."

She spoke of darkness and sleep as of cause and effect. But sleep did not come as easily and inevitably as that, and darkness often gave a spur to the thoughts by blotting out distractions.

He lay awake, still thinking of God's lights: of primrose street lamps, and garish neon signs, and the dragon eyes of motor cars. The Christmas lights would still be blazing in Henry Street, and the great colored advertisements in O'Connell Street would be flashing and dimming and spelling out words interminably in crimson and green and gold. And all these lights were His as surely as autumn skies and orange blossoms. There were no man-made lights. The things that were Caesar's were not really Caesar's. Everything came from the Man Above. He drew all the blueprints, and looked over the shoulders of the planners. Toothbrushes and submarines were his, sleeping pills and radar, polar bears and teddy bears. Bathing caps and electric drills were no different from dogfish, and television was simply a putting together of components that God had hidden under stones.

The city was full of lights, but they would be quenched in an hour or two. Janitors would lock up theaters and cinemas, and turn the last switches. The great flaring neon signs would flash once again and then go to sleep. In the end there would be nothing left but the street lights, and the city would wear darkness like a cloak until the day seeped in at the rim of the east.

It would be time then for ancient and enduring lights, for lights that were older than the catacombs, for the candles that never had gone out. He lay awake, thinking of Masses; of Masses timing the dawn from east to west around the bulge of the globe. The Canon went on and on, and Calvary was forever. Christ ever living and ever dying. The annihilation of wheat and sweet wine.

He lay awake, following the sun and the lighting of candles, listening to an endless Confiteor, watching sleepy men fixing ribbons in Missals and sleepy acolytes struggling into surplices. He prayed for the quick and the dead, and bracketed them together . . . for all here present and for all faithful Christians living and dead . . . and for many not so faithful. You could squeeze in all of Adam's children. Praying for one, you did him no hurt if you got him to move up and make room for all who had died in the French Revolution, and at Hiroshima and Vimy Ridge; for all who were buried in plague pits and convent cemeteries; for all who were snoring, or sinning, or praying, or paring their corns, or studying accountancy, or giving birth, or playing billiards, or moldering in the quiet earth.

It was a sharing that did not diminish. Each heir was the sole heir. You could pray for all these, and then, as an afterthought, throw in the seventeenth century, and Indonesia, and the American Navy, Martin Luther and the insurgents of 1798, the Church of Christ Scientist and the supporters of Real Madrid.

*   *

154 .

Brother Hilary, of all people, called to see him the following evening: Hilary the pocket religious, with his tiny head and blue eyes and pippin cheeks.

"Hilary! Where in the name of Cromwell did you come from. Man dear, I'm glad to see you. But I thought that you would have been back in England long before this."

Hilary's blue eyes flashed once, like bulbs on a midget Christmas tree, and dulled again.

"For a while it was touch and go if I'd ever go back. I got flu, and it developed into a spot of congestion. They pumped me full of wonder drugs at ten bob a shot, and here I am . . . They've moved you, I see."

"Aye, they said I'd be quieter here. But tell me about yourself. Are you feeling better?"

"Oh, yes. I'm ready for the road now."

"It was good of you to come, Hilary."

"And it was the devil's own job. First the Prior was for keeping me in. Said I shouldn't overtax myself. Then there was that wee nun at the door. She wasn't for letting me in at all. It would be nearly as easy to get an audience with the Pope."

"Sister Teresa?"

"I don't know what her name is, but she's a holy terror. 'Visitors are strictly forbidden,' says she. 'I'm not a visitor,' says I, 'and if I don't see him now I mightn't have the chance of seeing him for another ten years, and it's a hundred to one we'll both be dead before then.' "

"What did she say to that?"

" 'Only five minutes,' says she, 'and don't excite him.' 'Do I look very exciting?' says I, 'And as for the lad in the bed above he's as placid as a cow in a meadow.' "

"How did she take it?"

" 'Rules are rules,' says she, 'and they're made for the good of the patient, but in the circumstances I'll let you see him for five minutes' . . . There's a card on your door, by the way."

"What does it say?"

" 'No Visitors,' and 'Please do not feed the chimpanzee without the permission of the keeper.' "

"I had another turn, you know. They anointed me."

Hilary nodded his head.

"So I heard. They anointed me too. That makes two of us. Maybe I should be going. I'm over my time, and I don't want that one at the door to tackle me on the way out."

"Och, stay where you are. Her bark is worse than her bite."

"Is there anything you want?"

"Not a hait. Except maybe a glass of sherry or a raspberry ice or a few Hafner's sausages."

"Anything else? You wouldn't like my autograph or the Statue of Liberty?"

"I want to get into my trousers and get my heels with me out of this place. I'd like to get home for Christmas and go to the market to buy sprouts."

I'll never see him again, Bernard was thinking; nor he me. Aloud he said: "How are things beyond?"

"Same as ever. The Prior is still at his book."

Bernard reached under the pillow for a handkerchief. "The Prior, God bless him, has been writing a book since the year o' one, and he'll be writing it till the Lord calls him, whether that's soon or late."

"He's a simple man."

"And a holy man, Hilary. Barrin' myself he's the nearest thing to a saint we have in the house."

Hilary leaned back, balancing the chair on its hind legs.

"Saints are useful things to have about a house, but hard to live with. We had a saint in Cambridge when I was there—Brother Kevin—and he did us a powerful lot of good. He was as irritating as a hair shirt. A house without something in the line of a saint is in a bad way."

Their talk had no substance in it. They knew each other's minds and they had little need for talking. They had been young together, and now they were old. They had entered the novitiate on the same day, Bernard remembered: the big man from the mountains and the little man from the plains. They had prayed together and played together, and they were closer than kinsmen. They had done the same work in different places: looking after candles and vestments, cooking cabbage and bacon, setting up Christmas Cribs and putting washers on taps.

"Ever back a horse now, Hilary?"

This was an old joke, one of the stock jokes of the novitiate. Hilary was a good religious, but he might easily have been a good jockey. He had the hands for it and the weight. He had grown up in the Curragh, and horses were in his blood. Two of his brothers had been jockeys. They must be old men by now, old men with wizened faces.

"A fiver once in a while, Bernard, and maybe a pony on the Grand National. I don't have much money to spare nowadays."

The old jokes had lost their savor. There was no magic in them any more. Not that it mattered. They were old men, and what mattered was being together. There was so little time left.

157 .

"I must go this time, Bernard. That woman below will have my life if I stay any longer."

"Say a prayer for me then. When are you going back?"

"Tomorrow. I'm going by air. The Prior said it would be less tiresome. I never flew before."

"Well, you couldn't start any younger. You'll be home for Christmas."

"I will, thank God. And maybe you will be too, with a bit of luck."

Bernard shook his head. "I'm afraid not. But soon after, with the help of God."

It was quiet after Hilary's going, but it was good to have had him, even for a little while.

Hilary might have been a jockey, and Bernard might have been a police-man. Hilary might have exercised horses in the misty Curragh dawns, and kept his weight down with Turkish baths; Bernard might have worn a helmet and carried a baton, like his cousin Maurice Roarty of Meentagh.

Maurice had joined the Royal Irish Constabulary, and he had risen in the Force; first constable, then sergeant, and finally head constable. That was as far as a ranker could go normally, and very few of them got any further. To become an inspector you had to begin as a cadet, with breeding to back you.

Maurice was an enormous man, with the shoulders of a bison. He was well over six feet, and even as a young man he walked with a slow, deliberate gait and never answered a question until he had pondered it carefully. He looked like the makings of a policeman long before he went to the depot.

There was no brilliance in Maurice. He was slow, thorough, and dependable. He was intelligent, he kept the rules, and he knew the regulations by heart. He bludgeoned his way into promotion.

Most years, on his way north for his holidays, or on his way back again, he called to St. Michael's. Looking at him, Bernard saw himself as he might have been. And yet, not quite that, for there was no adaptability in Maurice, no compromise. He was fixed and constant in his beliefs and loyalties. He looked to the permanence of the things that were, and he had none of the resilience that takes the shock of change.

The times passed Maurice out, and left him, in the end, stranded and bewildered like a gasping fish. "There's no respect for a policeman now," he used to say to Bernard. "No respect at all. I don't know what madness has come over the people. There are fools drilling in every field and marching the roads with slouch hats. And the poor amaudans think they can tumble Buckingham Palace by forming fours and doing arms drill with wooden guns. God look to their wit! They are setting themselves against the might of the British Empire, but it will be there when they are dead and gone."

Maurice's faith in the British Empire was a long time crumbling, and when it went completely it brought his wits with it.

Bernard too had the makings of a policeman. He was six feet one in his stockinged feet, he turned the scale at fifteen stone, and he had as much rote learning as the next. He could name the Tudor monarchs, and the islands of the Baltic, and the rivers flowing into the White Sea. He was fool proof on Lord Roberts, and the Indian Mutiny, and Warren Hastings. He could do square root and compound interest and the theorem of Pythagoras. He had gone to Master Friel's night school and sat with big men who could recite "Cork, Queenstown, Fermoy, Youghal, Kinsale, Mallow, and Bandon."

"You could pass for the police with your eyes shut," Master Friel told him once. "If you don't pass first class I'll eat my dictionary." But Bernard did not sit for the depot entrance examination. Bernard stayed at home, but Maurice joined the constabulary, and Bernard listened to him year after year at holiday time and watched him grow old, and puzzled, and embittered, and resentful.

The history of Maurice was the history of his time and generation. He grew up in a time of peaceful agitation, and he grew old in a transition period which sharpened into a resurgence, the significance and purpose of which escaped him completely at first. Later on, its meaning became clear, but even then he closed his eyes to it and preferred his own early diagnosis to the reality, until in the end the madness that he had ascribed to those about him became first his agony and then his refuge and retreat.

Maurice spent six months in the Phoenix Park depot with other men like himself: big men all of them, and with the strength of the fields in their limbs. They wheeled and marched on the barrack square, they learned how to handle carbines and evildoers, and they memorized the rubrics of police law. Then they were posted to Courtmacsherry, or Oughterard, or Creeslough, or Tinahealy, but never to their own home counties—lest the ties of blood and kinship take the edge off their zeal and come between them and duty.

They came home on holiday wearing blue serge suits and silver watchchains, and usually with a bottle of whiskey in their luggage. They shook hands with everyone after Sunday Mass, they visited the neighbors, they sat stiffly and respectably at peaty firesides. They were accepted everywhere as men of substance and rectitude, as knowing fellows who had sovereigns in their pockets and the sign of their meat on them, as lucky ones who had fought free of the clabar and the hardship and were earning good money for doing sweet damn all.

They were majestic, solemn, mannerly. They listened and said little. They weighed their words, and spoke with the authority of experience. And the fact that they were King's men did not count against them in the least—except with cranky fellows like old Pat Maigey, who was an old Fenian and had a loaded stick hidden in his loft; for it was to King and Parliament that people looked for the redress of land grievances, and new piers, and money for roads, and a measure of self-government. The fight was in Westminster, not on the hillsides. It was a time of speeches and meetings, addresses and remonstrances, lobbying and hoping, a time for peaceful agitation and uneasy loyalty.

A generation was to pass before the gun came into its own again, and then it was only the young who wore leggings and bandoliers, and drilled in the gloaming, and remembered Forty-Eight—and only a handful of the young at that. For most of the young sided with the old and the middle-aged, who shook their heads and shrugged their shoulders and foretold disaster. Nothing good could come of this lunacy. Constitutional agitation was the only hope for Home Rule and better times and the land for the people. The Empire was as steady as a rock. Wooden guns would not shake it, and baiting it would do no good. The Empire was sprawled over the seven seas. It dyed the atlas red. It was impregnable and eternal.

The new movement gained strength but slowly at first, until Easter Week flared and died. That should have been the end, but it was only the beginning. And then it was not only the young who sided with the dreamers. The new movement had come of age. It was no longer the folly of youth but the anger of a whole people.

Maurice lived through it all, learning nothing, forgetting nothing, accepting nothing, and every time he passed through Dublin, he aired his resentment to Bernard.

"What folly is on them?" he would say, as he laid his cape and cap on a chair in the visitors' parlor. "Why can't they leave things the way they were? We were enjoying peace and plenty until they took to the gun. And Home Rule was as good as won. But now you're not an Irishman at all unless you side with them and turn a blind eye to their doings. It's a tough life being a policeman in these times."

It was tough, and it got tougher. The time came when Maurice could no longer come openly and in uniform, when he came like a conspirator, looking behind him over his shoulder, and starting at every footstep. In the end he gave up going north for his holidays, for now he got a cold welcome in his own parish and there was a hard look in men's eyes. He would come to Dublin for a day or two,

163 .

wondering at the strange turn of events which had made him an outcast in his own land and among his own people. And almost to the end he believed that those who had taken to the gun would see the foolishness of their ways, and that the day would come again when a policeman could walk the roads without fear of the bullet.

Most of the police had divided minds. They had joined the police in times when it was no shame to wear the uniform and when being a King's man had meant no more than issuing summonses for straying cattle or fraudulent weights, keeping a watch on unlighted bicycles and sheep-worrying dogs, and bringing "persons of the itinerant class" to the lock-up after the dispensary doctor had stitched up their unfeeling heads. But things had changed. Now the police were expected to spy on their own, to keep their ears to the ground, and to help to crush a movement that was beyond crushing.

In their time they had had easy lives. They had patrolled solemnly and needlessly, touching their caps to the priest and the parson, saluting the gentry, and saying, "That's a fine bit of an evening, thanks be to God" to farmers' daughters and district nurses and junior assistant mistresses. They had watched the corn ripen, and heard the Angelus ring, and fished in mountain streams. They had lived in a quiet land which serious crime seldom disturbed and criminals were as scarce as eclipses. Their police work was light. They arrested an odd drunk and disorderly, gave sonorous evidence at the Petty Sessions, and entered up portentuous nothings in the barrack day book.

They had the life of Reilly, the people said, and they enjoyed it while it lasted. They stood at corners in the long summer gleamings, shaved and shining, with their eyes fixed on the middle distance (but missing nothing that happened in the vicinity of Flaherty's pub) and their thumbs tucked between their stomachs and their polished black belts. A poteen raid was an event, and the capture of a still a red-letter day.

They were part of the community. They courted, and married, and reared children. They were good husbands and good fathers, and they held their heads high.

But all that had changed. Now they were alone and isolated. They neither greeted nor were greeted. They got black looks even from their own children; for those who had been reared in the odor of loyalty and on the King's bounty were not immune from this strange and terrible thing that had begun as a cloud no bigger than a man's hand but had grown and spread until the country was full of marching men. The country was full of marching men, and only the police were out of step.

Death walked the roads with them and every man's hand was against them. And they were concerned no longer with straying cattle or noxious weeds. They had more perilous work to do now, and their hearts were not in it. For they had not changed. They were still the big decent men who had walked the quiet roads and assessed the height of the growing corn. And now they were leagued of necessity with the Black-and-Tans, whom they detested, and who, with good reason, trusted them less than did the stern-faced men in leggings and trench coats who lived dangerously, and crossed the hills in the dawn, and dug holes in the roads, and tossed homemade grenades into Crossley tenders.

165 .

The police met the situation in various ways. Some of them resigned, and left the military to do their own work. Some of them stayed on and became the eyes and ears of the flying columns. Some did all that was asked of them. And some, like Maurice, did as little as they could whilst remaining outwardly loyal and co-operative. These last chose the hardest way, for they were in danger from both sides and were not fully trusted by either. Maurice stayed, for several reasons; because police work was the only trade he knew; because he did not want to spoil the thrift of a lifetime and forfeit his pension; and because he could never bring himself to believe that the old order had gone forever.

Maurice did not move with the tide. He never realized fully, even in the end, that the impossible had come to pass and that a handful of men with a dream in their hearts had moved the spirit of a nation. He refused to accept the reality, and he clung to the wild hope that the old days would come back until his mind weakened under the deception.

He retired on pension at the height of the "Trouble," and came to live in Dublin. But he was still islanded and isolated. He was a man apart, a brooding lonely soul, living his own life, thinking his own thoughts, stubborn, frightened, and fatalistic. No one had ever fired a shot at him, no one wanted his blood, but he fought with shadows to the end and they were with him till he died.

St. Michael's was his only port of call, and Bernard his only confidant. "If they knew that I was an ex-policeman," he used to say, "my life wouldn't be worth a thraneen. I'm never easy in

166 .

my own mind, and how could I be? If the lads below in Cork knew that I was here my days would be numbered. I never did more than I had to do, and sometimes I didn't even do that itself, for I hated the riffraff I had to work with, but that wouldn't save me if they knew where I was. If the Cork lads trace me here I'll be a marked man."

But the Cork lads had more to bother about, and the whole world knew that he was an ex-policeman. Unmistakably, he was that and nothing else. His bulk and his height and his gait were signs that no one could miss, and the very way that his clothes hung on him was a pointer. Not that it mattered one way or another, for no one was hounding or trailing him. He might have lived in peace, but his poor mind gave him no rest, and he practiced little subterfuges that were as futile as they were unnecessary. He walked with a stoop that merely accentuated the height it was intended to disguise, and every time he changed his lodgings—and he changed them every couple of months—he told his landlady that he was a re-tired school inspector. But fear was always at his heels, and he lived in a dark world of his own mak-ing.

Bernard watched him deteriorate. He developed nervous twitches, he spun round in his chair at the slightest sound, and he champed his jaws on thoughts to which he gave no utterance.

On his last visit to the monastery there was a wild look in his eyes.

"I'm going, Bernard. I can't stand it any longer."

"Going where, Maurice?"

"London, Glasgow, Edinburgh, anywhere out of this cursed country. I'll clear out and go some-

167 .

where where nobody will know me. I might have some peace then, but I have none now. I'll clear out, I tell you."

"Nonsense, man. If they wanted you, they would have got you long before this. And why would anyone want to lay a hand on you? Sure you never harmed anyone."

Maurice locked his hands together with a fierce and pitiful pressure. Then he loosened them again and stood up. He was like a prophet of old.

"You don't understand. Nobody understands. But I know they're after me. They've been after me ever since I came to Dublin. They're just waiting their chance. Everywhere I go I see people looking at me."

"They look at me too, Maurice. You're imagining things."

But there was no reasoning with him. He might have been alone and speaking to himself.

"Last night, on the quays, I passed two young fellows with Cork accents. This morning when I was leaving the digs I saw them again. It'll be the gun for me if I don't go soon. That's the God's truth. I'll be safer far in London."

He would have been safe anywhere, and the only danger that threatened was in his poor twisted mind.

"Goodbye, Bernard. Don't say a word to anyone. They have ears everywhere. If anyone asks about me, say that you don't know where I am."

Bernard made a last effort.

"Listen, Maurice. You'd be miserable in London. Stay here. Mix with people. Talk to people. Go out more. You're too much wrapped up in yourself."

Maurice reached for his hat. "That's foolish talk. Don't you realize that I'm a hunted man?"

And it was the simple truth. Maurice was a hunted man, and Bernard had another one to pray for.

Maurice wrote once after his going to London. He gave no address, and the letter was unsigned. He was still trying to cover up his tracks.

The next news of him came from a doctor in a London mental hospital, saying that Maurice Roarty was a patient there and that Bernard's name and address had been found in a slip of paper in his pocket. The prognosis was not favorable.

A year later, the doctor wrote again. Maurice had gone from the world of shadows, and his poor tortured spirit was at peace.

Christmas was only five
days away. Bernard awoke from a doze to see
Sister Augustine taking the covers off electro-
plated dishes. Soup, roast chicken, apples and
custard; and afterwards the red-faced, flip-floppy
wardsmaid would bring him tea and biscuits. They
were feeding him like a fighting cock.

"Now, that's a fine dinner," said Sister Augustine.

"I could do with a worse one if I were out of
this place. I'm tired here."

"Shame on you, Brother. You should be thank-
ing God for all his goodness. You're making good
progress."

"I'm feeling fine, but I'm lonely here. There
was more fun downstairs, and more chat."

"Quietness is better for you. And sure you can always talk to yourself, and say your prayers."

"I do both betimes, ma'am . . . Did I ever tell you what Billy Eamuinn said to the nun in the county home?"

Augustine said nothing. She stood waiting.

"Billy was a great man for stories, but he let his farm go to loss, and he finished up in the county home. He was never short of an answer, and the nuns were always quizzing him.

"One day, one of them said to him, 'Did you ever know, Billy, that I was married?' 'Troth then I did not,' says Billy. 'Who were you married to?' 'I'm married to Our Lord,' says she. 'Be dammits, then,' said Billy, 'but you married into a dacent family.' "

Augustine pretended to be shocked. "I'm ashamed of you, Brother," she said. "Such a story to tell!"

"Billy had a sister named Sheila," went on Bernard, "and they never agreed. It was more Billy's fault than hers, for he was always behind with his farm work and the house was falling to bits.

"When Mary died, and her corpse was lying down in the room, some of the neighbors called to sympathize with Billy. 'You lost Mary,' one of them said to him. 'If I did,' says Billy, 'I lost neither thrift nor wisdom, but degradation, temptation, and desolation.' "

"You're an awful man!" said Augustine. "I often wonder had you a vocation at all."

"I often wondered about it myself, ma'am."

But he hadn't wondered. He hadn't wondered at all. The thought had been in his mind for a long,

171 .

long time. It was not a summons or a call or a warning. It was rather a quiet reminder, constantly repeated; and with it was the conviction that it would not be repeated indefinitely.

It dated from the evening he had gone fishing with Father Dan in the Big Burn. It had been no more than a feeling then, something vague and indefinite which he could not match with words. But gradually it became clearer and more insistent. It was not constant. It came and went; and it came in the strangest places; at a wake in Crawford's of Clondrohid, when the body of old Sandy Crawford was cold in the lower room, and the kitchen was full of tobacco smoke and high spirits; coming home from a dance in Meentagh, when the moon sparkled on the ice in the road-side ruts and the hills wore white shawls; in the high moss, when he was trundling a loaded barrow and the sweat was running from him.

He could banish it at times, like an unquiet thought; and there were times too when he felt it was gone forever. But it kept coming back. There was no sense of compulsion in it, no feeling of fate. He was being offered a choice, but he was as free as the wind.

For a long time he sought no advice, for Father O'Loughlin was the only one whom he could consult, and he never felt at ease with Father O'Loughlin. It was during a Mission that he spoke of it first. Missions were big events in the Glen. They came only once in five years or so. The missioners were known as "the holy fathers," as if they were little popes. A thundering missioner —and many of them thundered—could put the fear of God into you. But there were quiet missioners too, and it was to a quiet one that he spoke: a

Franciscan with a tiny head and the face of an ascetic.

Bernard bided his time. He shrunk from going to the parochial house. A visit there would be noticed and would lead to conjecture. And he did not want to unburden himself at Confession, since that would mean spending a long time in the box and coming out red-faced to meet the meaningful looks of the other penitents. He waited until the priest was taking the air on the road outside the church after a long spell of "hearing."

The priest listened quietly, saying nothing at all at first. He was a man you could speak to. You felt that he grasped the half-said thing.

"I see, my son," he said at last. "Well, don't worry about it. Take your time and say your prayers. If you feel the same way in six months' time you could go ahead. Have you ever thought of being something else, of staying in the world, that is?"

"Often, Father. I thought of going to Glasgow or the States. And I had a notion of joining the police."

The priest answered very quietly. There was a smile on his lips. "And now you have a notion of becoming a lay brother, and you want to know whether it is only a notion or something stronger. That is why you must pray. This is a thing on which you must make up your own mind.

"I won't advise you one way or another. I think you would make a good religious, but a lay brother's life is not an easy one. It needs a special vocation. More lay brothers than priests have been raised to the altars of the Church. That's something to think about.

"Don't rush things. Pray for light and guidance.

173 .

Pray especially to the Holy Ghost. Write to me any time you feel like it. In the meantime, pray for me and I'll pray for you. We'll swap prayers."

Bernard didn't wait six months. He had put off his decision for a long time, but when he made it he made it quickly and irrevocably.

One day, about six weeks after his talk with the missioner, he brought a load of peats to Derryleigh and hawked it round the town. They were good peats, crisp and dry as biscuits but he had the devil's own job selling them, and in the end he had to let them go to a coast guard's wife for six shillings. It was a poor price for a load of peats, for peats that had to be cut, and footed, and turned, and stacked, and drawn; a poor price for toil and sweat. But when you brought a load of peats to Derryleigh you didn't bring it home with you again. You sold in a buyer's market and you took what you got. Six shillings was poor pay, but it was better than nothing.

He bought a shop loaf, an ounce of tobacco for his father, and a bag of bull's eyes for his mother. Then he set out for home.

On his way out of the town he left the mare at the chapel gate and walked up the sloping, sanded path. In the porch he took Holy Water from the bowl that nestled in the top of a low wooden pillar. When he walked up the aisle the noise of his stiff, iron-tipped boots was like thunder. There was silence all about him, and coolness, and a faint smell of incense and beeswax.

As he genuflected (and he did it with the stiff knee-jerk that was traditional in the Glen—he had to learn to genuflect properly when he went to the novitiate), he noticed that the sanctuary lamp had gone out. Lighted, it was like a living heart; unlit, it chilled the spirit. It was as if God had withdrawn Himself.

Halfway up the aisle he knelt down on the edge of the seat and blessed himself. He had not come for any special purpose, beyond making a visit and saying a few prayers, but before he got to his feet again the decision had been taken. There was no emotion in the moment, no elation, no rush of sentiment. A question had been answered, a problem resolved, an invitation accepted. Never before had he been so conscious of the fact that the decision was wholly his own, and that he was free to go one way or the other.

He left the chapel, splashed himself with Holy Water in a habit sequence, and walked down the path to the gate in the curved wall, lurching a little with the slope. Below him lay the wide Lough, and beyond it, stretching inland and seaward, was a great backbone of mountains. Beside the chapel, in a hilly field dotted with yellow benweeds, a calf was lowing with a comforting, pagan sound. The rattle and crunch of the wheels, when the cart moved off again and he gave the mare her head, had the same quality. This was the world of beast-smell and clay-smell, of spittle and corduroy, of gear and harness, of soda scones and stable cleaning, of blue smoke and white walls. It was the world he knew; the world he knew and loved.

A man could be happy enough here, thinning turnips and drawing peats, leaving a tide-mark under his nose when he slugged strong tea from a patterned bowl, mixing copper sulphate and soda when the white blossoms and the blue blossoms were in the potato fields. He could have days of quiet labor, and at night he could warm his shins at a neighbor's fire and listen to the chat of the seven townlands. He could sleep in his shirt under a patchwork quilt that reeked of turf smoke, listening to the rattle of chains from the byre, and the sleepy stirrings of fowl, and the beat of the waves at Bun na dTonn. It was an ordered world where the pattern of life repeated itself endlessly, where one day was like another, and where the sequence was as satisfying as the turns the ear listened for in a well-known tune.

A man could be happy enough here, and not too far from God. He would slump down on the earthen floor every night, dangle his beads against the legs of his chair, and say his decade in his turn. He would listen to the old folk mumbling prayers from which long habit had rubbed the edges of intelligible sound, and stretching out the trimmings to the Rosary.

At the Kinegar, a rabbit crossed the road, flaunting its white scut like a cockade and looking back once before it vanished in the ferns; and lower down, at the turn near the graveyard, where the road corkscrewed uphill between ancient walls and was roofed with tall trees, a snake-headed weasel flowed into a crack in the stone. He was to remember that evening. Many a time in the years that followed he travelled it again, and the road unrolled in his mind like a film.

At McBride's forge, where he turned inland and left the Lough for a while, the sweet, heavy scent of woodbine came to him from the tangle of bush and briar at the foot of the mountain, and an early corncrake began its hoarse lament. He was in bare country then, with great stretches of moorland on either side of him, and thin funnels of grey smoke seeping up from the scattered townlands. The

176.

road moved upward all the way, sometimes over steep braes, sometimes by long, almost imperceptible slopes, till it reached the turn of Croc Ard. The Glen always took you by surprise, for until you reached the very edge of the slope the hills on the far side seemed a continuation of the road on which you were travelling; and then, suddenly, you looked down on the Glen that Croc Ard and Cnoc Eala shepherded to the Lough, and you saw the toy houses and the chapel and the yellow cornfields, and the squat granite headlands that faced the northern sea.

This was his own country, and it had never looked lovelier than on this evening when he had decided to leave it forever. Leaving it was no longer an escape. It was a giving, a surrender, a sundering.

He was glad then that he had something to give. It took all selfishness out of his going. There was another thought too that was present to his mind in a dim way but became clearer and more meaningful with the years. To balance places like the Glen—and places, too, like Boston and Glasgow —there had to be outposts manned by dedicated people who had foresworn home and kin. There had to be someone on guard. The Glen blessed itself morning and night, and gathered to Mass on Sundays; for the rest, like all the world, it prayed by proxy. The corn had to be reaped and the hay stooked, but it was just as necessary that prayer should rise unceasingly to the God of homes and harvests. Coal came up from the maw of the earth, and raw steel hulks slipped down the runways to the sea, but somewhere, and all the time, there had to be folk on their knees. The profession of prayer was an essential part of spiritual economy.

And even in monasteries the same economy held. Some chanted in choir, and others kept the scones from burning. Missions had to be manned in distant places, but the spuds had to be peeled and the parlor floor waxed. The preacher in the pulpit depended on men who wore the same habit and stirred pots in the kitchen. The man who brought the Holy Oils to the dying shared his reward and privilege with the man who roasted the herrings he would eat on his return.

He stood for a while at the turn of Croc Ard and let the mare crop the sweet grass by the roadside. Beneath him was the whole stretch of the Glen, with its ribbon roads and cropped fields and purple moorlands. Every chimney, every blaze of white rock, every clump of bushes was a familiar landmark. This was where he had been born, and he knew it like the back of his hand. He could have closed his eyes and plotted every perch of it. This was the Glen, the last outpost of Ireland, the end of a road that led to nowhere. It was a lost and lonely place, a lost and lovely place, and it caught at his heart.

The gloaming thickened as he stood, and the lighthouse on the far side of the Lough began to blink sleepily. Then a few scattered lights appeared in the Glen, glimmering like stars new-kindled. He could put a name on every one of them: Deeneys of Ardsbeg, O'Donnells of Creeve, Cullions of Upper Drumbane. This was his own country, and these were his own people. He could tell any man in it two furlongs off by his build and gait, and if he met a new scholar on his way to the school he could name him by his freckles and coloring.

He knew then that leaving the Glen did not mean cutting adrift from it forever. It had molded and made him, and he would bring it with him wherever he went. It had colored his thoughts and his speech, it was part of the idiom of his mind, and it would be with him to the end of his days.

He thought of Master Friel's lessons on history. "A country is too big to know at first," he used to say. "You must begin with something smaller—a hillside, a townland, a parish, a county. You love what you know. Patriotism is a series of widening circles. Love of country is a reaching out from the place where you were born." And that was only half the story. A townland was nothing but the people in it, and a parish was a register of family names.

He felt chilled after a while. He took the mare by the head and led her down the steep slope, staunching his feet against the fall of the road. When he reached level ground again he climbed into the cart and gave the mare her head. She broke into a steady trot, not just because the light cart was no burden to her, or because she was done with hills, but because she had left all strangeness behind her and was near the lane that led home.

Years afterwards, when he thought of that evening, he found it hard to distinguish between the thoughts that had belonged to it and the later thoughts that had overlain it. For it was the source of all that followed. It was a vigil and a dedication. When the stars came out, and darkness covered the face of the Glen, the night came on like a prayer.

Next morning, he broke the news to his mother. In one way, it was hard telling her, for in the Glen the things of the heart were seldom put into words, and the love of children and parents was taken for granted. In another, it was easy enough. She was a Glenswoman, and she knew that to rear children was to lose them. The count seldom varied: it was one for the plow and the rest for the stranger.

"A thaisge!" was all she said at first, and then her tears came. He could read her thoughts. She had assumed that she would lose him in due course to Philadelphia or Clydeside, or that he would wear belt and baton like Maurice Roarty, but this was something new in her experience, and mixed with the loneliness in her eyes there was wonder and happiness.

"You never told me. A thaisge?"

"I couldn't tell you till I was sure, and I wasn't sure until now."

"How long has this thing been in your mind?"

"For a long time now." And it was a long time. The cutting in the pocket of his Sunday suit that began *Young men of good character who wish to devote themselves to the service of God* was so tattered that it was barely legible.

"When will you be leaving us, son?"

"Maybe in a month or so. I'll have to write."

She sat down and wiped her eyes in her apron.

"I'm heartbroken and happy this minute," she said. "It'll be sore losing you, and we'll miss you, but we'll not grudge you to the Man you're going to. You'll take a blessing and you'll leave a blessing, and that will be a link between us forever."

He had no words to answer her. He put on his cap and went out to the end of the house, where he busied himself putting a new face on a turf stack that had been tumbled by the wind.

*　　*

He had fewer visitors in the upper room. Kilian, Paul, and the Prior came and went, but their visits were well spaced, and they never remained very long. Hilary had overstayed his leave, and Sister Teresa, apparently, had put her foot down.

Not that he minded very much. He had had no recurrence of his pain, and he knew that things were coming right at last. Besides, he was growing used to being alone, and he could draw his visitors from the past: Hughie and Father Dan; Maurice Roarty with his troubled, smoldering eyes; Sam Garnley and the Flapper Flanagan; Father Sebastian, and Brother Colum, and the long roll of the community's dead.

And he was thinking constantly of the Glen. He heard Master Friel calling the school roll—Tom Doherty, Lurgameelon, John Friel, Doaghbeg, William Gallager, the Brig. Faces, voices, and sounds came back to him: the faces of Manus the Shop and Denis the Sodger and Ned the Yankee; the sound of cows walking with high-heeled shoes in the stony lane that led to the hill parks; the sound of a man putting an edge on a scythe, the sound of a herder playing a tin whistle on the far side of the burn; smells, too: the smell of burning peat, and retting flax, the smell of the shore when the seaweed was ripe and bursting, the smell of homespun congregations.

He thought of the Logues, of his own kith and kin, of a great scattering of "friends"—first cousins, and second cousins, and second cousins once removed, of all who were sib to his own folk.

But soon there would be no more Logues in the house by the Big Burn. Kate and Barney and Ellen were in Philadelphia for donkey's years, and he heard from them only once in a blue moon. The

Logues of Ardsbeg would soon be done. Their day was almost over, their lease was running out. The only two left at home now were Tom and Mary, and they had neither chick nor child to follow them. Tom was as old as a bush, and Mary was not far behind him. The farm, for what it was worth, would go to Charlie Friel, a distant cousin who came over from Lurgameelon to do the ploughing and reaping, and who would sell the place as soon as he got his hands on it.

The Glen that Bernard knew was dead and gone. He had not been next or near it for years. Mary wrote to him at Christmas and Easter. Her eyesight was failing badly, and her copperplate had become a scrawl. She had nothing to tell him except that Tom was bad with rheumatics and that old Ned Dunleavy died last month. She was an old, spent woman, sitting by an empty hearth by the side of a done man.

But Bernard was glad of her letters. They brought back the past and linked him with his origins. Besides, when a man grew old he became fonder of his own folk and clung to the few that were left.

He had often wondered about the fate of the world, the parts of it that he knew and loved, and the parts which, like Salamanca and Rome and Cleveland, were his only by hearsay. Would it all shrivel up some day and even its embers vanish to nothing? Would all the loveliness of mountains and polar seas, of bazaar sounds and harvest smells, of hills and sunsets and clouds and distances—would all this be wiped out like a stain?

It seemed a desecration, a waste of God's handiwork. The earth was only a tiny incident in space, a speck in the infinite, but it was very dear to God

Almighty. Would He rub all out like a blackboard diagram when the lesson of life was over, or would He leave it for the delight of those who had seen too little of its beauty? Would old women who had lived in damp tenements and never strayed beyond the tether of the neighboring streets be given visas as glorified bodies and sent on thought-swift, instantaneous tours to Fuyijama and Table Mountain and the head waters of the Amazon? Would they leap like fawns through space and learn in a flash all of chemistry and physics and mathematics so that they could time the flash and fall of meteors and comets and plot the changes in the polar icecap?

It was an old old fancy of his, and he had aired it once or twice to Father Austin. Austin was one of the clever ones. He was a physicist as well as a theologian. He had degrees from Louvain and Rome, and he knew his onions. It was a poor compliment to God Almighty, Austin had said, to rate the earth as his masterpiece and a knowledge of its mechanics as a part of celestial bliss. God's measures were infinity and omnipotence. To gauge heaven by earth was to shrink Him.

But Austin, for all his learning, had not been dogmatic. Some things were of Faith, but, outside these, thought was free, and one man's guess was as good as another's. So Bernard clung to his thesis and found it comforting to think that the earth would not disintegrate until all the sons of Adam had sucked its wonders dry.

Austin's theology was at once simpler and more involved. Knowing God, you knew everything; seeing Him, you saw all that was; and outside Him there was nothing. To all this, Bernard assented in the measure of his understanding, submitting his own gapped thinking to the conclusions of wiser

183 .

heads. But he saw no inconsistency between loving God for Himself alone, and the primer stage of loving Him in the things He had made. The green earth was dwarfed by the stars, but God's thumbprint was on it. He had peopled the heavens with mighty worlds, and they sang His glory, but He had lived and died on one of the smallest of them and He loved it with a love that was human as well as divine. And it gave testimony of Him as surely as did the whirling constellations. It was no treason to love seas and cities; orchards in bloom, hills against the sun and the curving necks of horses; shape and color, mass and form, volcanoes and chrysanthemums; to link all things with their Source and glimpse the Maker in the thing made.

But now, lying in his upper room, he began to have doubts about his own theories. His love of the green earth and his reluctance to think of its being shrivelled up some day like a flea in a candle flame argued lack of trust and imperfect knowledge. In destroying, God did not destroy. Nothing impoverished Him, nothing augmented. His assets were infinite, His resource inexhaustible. If He took something away, He could replace it with something a million times more lovely, and even that would be no measure of His own loveliness.

16 .

It was three days before Christmas. The upper sky was blue and clear, and the midday sun was melting the frost from the roofs of the city.

Bernard's room was as neat as it could possibly be, but Sister Magdalena came in to make it still neater. She tugged at his bedclothes, moved the vase of flowers a fraction of an inch, and patted a cushion on a chair.

"Mr. Williamson will be here any minute."

"Is that it?" said Bernard. "I was wondering what had you so fussed and flustered."

The day was clear and bright, and Mr. Williamson, when he came, was a part of it. His grey hair was carefully brushed, and he smelt of shaving lotion. His well-cut suit flattered his girth. His handsome face showed care, concern, and optimism.

"Isn't that a wonderful day, Brother?"

"It is indeed, thanks be to God."

Mr. Williamson knew a lot about hearts. But he knew less about hearts than a plumber did about cisterns. The plumber had an advantage. He could climb up and look in and see for himself. All Mr. Williamson could do was to stand outside and listen.

He was listening now. When he had the earpieces of his stethoscope sticking out of his head like baby horns, he could assume a look of intense and passionate concentration. It did you good even to look at him.

"How am I doing, doctor?"

"Fine, you're doing very well indeed. Very well. I'm quite pleased." He said this as if Bernard were responsible for his own condition and had earned praise.

"When will I be getting out then? I'm sick, sore, and tired of lying here."

Mr. Williamson's handsome face clouded ever so slightly and cleared again almost at once. "Not this side of Christmas, I'm afraid. You must be patient. Say early in the new year."

"You mean that, doctor?"

"I don't see why not. Unless you have a setback, and I can't see any reason why you should."

"And I'll be all right?"

"As good as new—or almost. You'll have to be careful, of course, and not overdo things. You understand that, of course?"

Bernard nodded. He knew that a heart didn't heal like a broken leg, that it couldn't be staunched liked an ailing tooth, and that once it erupted it was like a sleeping volcano. He liked the thought of going back to St. Michael's, but he had no illusions. He would not be the Brother Bernard that was. He would be marked "Fragile—This Side Up" and they would treat him the way a woman treated her best china.

"Yes, you're coming along nicely," went on Mr. Williamson. "You can try out your legs as soon as you like. You're bound to feel a little weak and shaky at first, but don't be alarmed at that. After all, you've been a fair time in bed."

The things he reminds me of, Bernard was thinking.

"Walk about the room a little for a start, and take a rest as soon as you feel tired. Then when you get your sea legs you can take a turn in the corridor—so long as you're careful."

"I'll be careful," said Bernard.

That afternoon, he dressed himself in shirt and trousers, slippers and overcoat. It was slow going, and he sat on the edge of the bed for a while to get his breath. Then he hobbled round the room, journeying anxiously from support to support. It was good to feel his legs under him again and to know that they answered the helm. But he lurched and wobbled a bit, and he was conscious of his breathing.

He sat in the armchair for ten minutes and looked out at the city. In the bed it had seemed remote, but now he felt that he was a part of it. He was in circulation again.

He tried the corridor next, keeping close to the wall and taking baby steps. There were three other convalescents there, post-operative cases by the look of them. They were wrapped up like Buddhist monks and they walked on ice.

The oldest of them was a fat, middle-aged man with no hair and bad teeth. "It's tough learning to walk again," he said. "Years ago they kept you in bed after an operation. Now they have you on your feet at the first opportunity."

"I suppose the doctors know what they're doing, and anyway you'll be out all the sooner."

"I won't be out for Christmas, worse luck, and I don't like the prospect of spending it here. Gall-stones I'm in for. What's your trouble?"

"There I leave you. Something wrong with the heart, but they haven't put a name on it."

He saw the look of concern in the big man's eyes. It stayed barely long enough to make a liar of him.

"Ah, they can do wonderful things with the heart nowadays. It's nothing to worry about."

On his second turn up the corridor he met Sister Augustine at the top of the stairs. "Good man!" she said. "You're doing nicely. Would you like to see the Crib and the Christmas tree in the main hall? They're lovely."

"I suppose I might as well see the sights."

"I'll get Michael to bring you down in the lift."

"Tell me, Sister. Can I go down to Mass in the morning?"

"It might be wiser not to. Don't rush things. But I'll let you to Mass on Christmas Eve if you're good."

Michael arrived presently and linked him to the lift. Michael was taking no chances. He set him free in the lift, where he hadn't room to fall, but once they were on the level he took him in tow again.

The Crib in the hall was the cleanest of Cribs. You could have taken a straw at random and

188 .

cleaned your teeth with it. The Christmas tree was perfectly symmetrical, and its lights were spaced with mathematical precision. He thought of the St. Michael's Crib, which was his delight and his boast. He liked a touch of untidiness in a Crib, and he had always tried to avoid a tableau effect.

But it would be a tableau this year for once. Paul would carry in the figures, and drape the brown paper rock on the wooden frame, and ruffle the straw, but he would be no better than a plumber's mate. The Prior would be in charge. He would cock his head to one side and say "Perhaps if you moved Saint Joseph over a little." He would change one piece of holly for another, and then he would stand back to get the general effect and change his mind again. The Prior would make a right mess of the Crib. He would have it as regular and unreal as a display in a shop window. After all, no one arranged the decor of the Crib at Bethlehem. It just happened.

He knelt at the Crib for a few minutes. Michael knelt with him and rose when he rose. Michael had his orders.

"Will I bring you back now, Brother?"

"I suppose so, Michael."

He was linked back to the lift and hoisted to the top floor. Then he was escorted to his own room and delivered in good order and condition. Michael went out and closed the door behind him like a turnkey. He was alone then. The room was as small as a cell. He was as isolated as a Carthusian.

He undressed himself slowly and he was glad to be back between the sheets again. He felt tired suddenly. When he remembered that he had not gone near the chapel, he clawed under the pillow for his

189 .

beads. He prayed, but not for long. Formal prayers tired him now, and a round of the beads was as much as he could manage at a time.

On the locker-top there were some books from the hospital library. Three of them were detective novels. He had read through one of them—his first ever—but he had found it hard to remember clues and collate time sequences, and he had left the others unread. There was a spiritual book also, and although he had ploughed through it dutifully and in small doses he had found it heavy going. From now on, he thought, he would stick to the New Testament.

Not that he had ever had much time for reading, spiritual or secular. His place was not in the library or the study, and there were abler men to man the rostrums. His place was in the kitchen, with pots and pans, and in the workshop with saw and hammer. He mixed paints and put new cords in windows; he sprayed his apple trees and picked caterpillars off his cabbages; he mended tables and vestments. He chopped beef and washed potatoes and cooked dinners for doctors of canon law and up-and-coming theologians. He worked with his hands and left philosophy for those who were able for it and had need of it.

He had worked with his hands and prayed with his hands, never coming within an ass's roar of sanctity, and breaking the rule once in a while. But there was little strength left in his hands now. They were the hands of an old doddering man. They were great spreading hands, built for sore labor; but the meat had wasted from them and the blood moved sluggishly through their blue, corded veins. They had done good work in their time, now they could travel no further than the border of the eiderdown.

But there was no spancel on his mind. Thought spanned the world. The furthest stars were within its reach.

He was not bounded by the walls of his tiny room. There was no tether on him at all. He could look down from above and watch Paul nailing up holly for the Crib. He could hover above the green dome of the Four Courts and watch a Guinness barge nosing its way downstream and arrowing the surface of the dark river.

It was only a wing-beat from the Liffey to the Boyne Viaduct and the blue line of the Mournes, and after the orchards of Armagh you caught the silver gleam of the salmon-thronged Foyle and saw the flattened snakehead of Innishowen stretching out into the northern sea. You were in familiar territory then. You crossed the gash of the Swilly and saw the toy church of the Glen, the tufts of trees that marked the hidden townlands, and the head-landed bay where the Bun na dTonn boats were beached opposite the fort at Dunree that guarded the mouth of the Lough.

But there was no point in lingering in the Glen and looking down on an old man and an old woman warming their shins at a turf fire and thinking long. The Glen was empty now. There was nothing left in it but memories.

The smoke of Belfast gave you a line for Liverpool, the city that had swallowed up Hughie and many another like him. The Irish were strong in Liverpool, and if you headed due north to the furnaces and gantries of Clydeside you would find more of your race and breed. In and about Glas-

191 .

gow there were a hundred times as many Donegal folk as there were in the united parishes of Derryconneely, Ballygashel, and Oughterbuidhe—aye and with Fanad and the Rosses thrown in.

He had been in Lourdes once—unexpectedly, almost miraculously—because Flaherty the cattle man had offered a pilgrimage ticket for one of the community. He had been in Lourdes once, and the picture of it was still clear in his mind: the hilly streets, and the milling crowds, and the babble of tongues; shabby Italian priests, and loud-voiced German priests, and Spanish nuns with patched habits; the shops with their tinkling statues and hanks of beads, the interminable repetitions of the Lourdes hymn, the clamorous comings and goings.

But once you were inside the great enclosure, everything changed. The money-changers were barred from the temple. Here there was only prayer and supplication, and Masses on the heels of Masses, and the sick in their rickshaw chariots—God's aristocracy in their livery of suffering—and a weaving pattern of torches, and the silence of the Grotto at midnight. Nothing had been changed at the Grotto. The crutches had blackened with the years, the guttering candles boiled over untidily, the statue of the Blessed Virgin was a poor, simple statue. To go to Lourdes was to stay there always, to kneel forever at the shrine, to pray eternally with black folk and white folk and brown folk. Lourdes was God's city and Mary's city; in a pagan country, in a pagan continent, in a pagan world.

He could have given a lecture on Lourdes, but the rest he had to build up from things heard or read or seen—from pictures in magazines and the accounts given by travelled members of the community: Santiago, to which pilgrims had trudged

across the Pyrenees all through the centuries; Salamanca, the golden city where Father Dan had drunk
the red wine and dreamed of the Swilly country.
In Rome, where time and eternity met, the pilgrims
were thick in St. Peter's Square. Beyond Rome,
Greece and Cyprus and the footsteps of the apostles.

The map of Asia was blank in his mind, but he
could see half-naked men planting rice in flooded
fields, and a great tangle of boats on the Yellow
River. He remembered names like Siam and Bang-
kok and Pekin, but the names he remembered best
were names like Gallagher, and Friel, and O'Doherty, and to find these in bulk he had to cross the
Pacific. The clans were thinning out at home, but
they were still plentiful in Philadelphia and Boston.

Seen this way, it was a tiny world. You could
span it in less time than it took you to say a decade
of your beads, and cross it from west to east while
the dusk was falling. To get real space you had to
go up and up until the earth dwarfed to a spinning
gooseberry in a vast emptiness lit by the stars.

Father Austin knew all about the stars. He could
grade them and weigh them and count them. There
were a million million stars for every person on the
earth. Or perhaps it was only five million for every
person. Not that it mattered very much. The count
would be revised with every new telescope. If you
could move with the speed of light for ten years or
so you might reach a fair-sized star, and even then
you were only on the fringe of outer space. Beyond you forever were myriad constellations moving outward into infinite distance. It was lonely up
there. If you could dig yourself in for a million
years on your first star you might see light from
some of the outliers arrowing past you on its way
to the earth.

193 .

He opened his eyes to familiar things, to near and comforting things; chairs and walls, bed and wash basin. But perhaps they were not so near, perhaps they were not so comforting, and they were certainly not solid. Austin could wean you from that heresy. The wood of the bedside cabinet and the porcelain of the basin were full of emptiness. All that seemed solid was riddled with vast, sky-lonely spaces, and every space was a hollow firmament housing infinitesimal bodies that moved in ordained orbits. Nothing was at rest, nothing was static. Everything was a universe in itself, small or big accordingly, as you looked at it. You could reach infinity both ways, and yet never reach it, and if you boggled at the stars you could not swallow apple pips.

And everywhere was God. He was in every molecule as truly as he was in Orion. He was in the telescope and the star and the eye behind the eyepiece. He charted every light ray and decided when every wave would break and crumble. All power, all movement was His continuing gift.

You bent before Him, and then you stood up and claimed kinship with Him. You said "Your Son, our Lord." You begged that by the mystery of this wine and water you might be made a partaker in His divinity as He had deigned to be a partaker in your humanity. And you were not speaking figuratively. You were stating a historical fact, for Christ had taken a created body, and a created soul. In the face of this tremendous mystery the problems of meteors and molecules were kindergarten exercises.

194.

17

Another day had come and gone. It was the eve of Christmas Eve. Kilian was with him in the little room. He had come laden with brown-paper parcels.

"You're spoiling me," Bernard told him. "This luxury isn't in the Rule. It's still Advent, you know."

"For the time being you're outside rules and regulations. And you'll be back with us soon, I believe."

"Early in the new year, the doctor says. I don't like the idea of spending Christmas in here."

"You could be in many a worse place."

"True enough."

And he might easily have been in a better. It had been touch and go with him twice. He had been to the brink and back.

"You won't feel the time passing, Bernard. To-morrow will be a busy day for us all, but you'll have your fill of us on Christmas Day."

Kilian had all the news of the monastery, and it was comforting to listen to him. It was news from home. And he would be back there again soon himself . . . But he would have to re-learn old tricks. He had been too long in the shadows, and he would have to get used to the light again. Perhaps Lazarus had felt like that too.

"They're letting me up for Mass tomorrow. I was up for a while yesterday, and I'll get up for a few hours after dinner today."

"You're home and dried, Bernard. Home and dried."

"If I'm not home soon you'll have to mortgage the place beyond. I must be costing more than Colman brings in."

The day moved on. Kilian went, and the little wardsmaid arrived with silverplated dishes. Lunch was a lucky dip. You lifted the covers, and then you knew. It was different in St. Michael's, where you chose the food and washed it and cooked it. Here it was revealed at the last minute, like a conjuring trick.

"Well, Siobhan. How are you today?"

"Fine, thanks, Brother. And yourself?"

"Threshing, child. Threshing. I suppose you'll be going home for Christmas?"

"Not this year. Some of us have to stay." She was a stocky, red-faced girl, awkward in her movements and a little sulky looking. "But I don't mind very much," she went on. "I'll be leaving for good in March."

"Leaving?"

196 .

She nodded. "I'm going to a hospital in England. There's more money there."

"But you might be happier here?"

"That's what my mother says. The old folk don't like to see us going. But sure everyone is going to England these days. The work is easier and the pay is better. There are five girls from home in a hospital near Birmingham. I won't be lonely."

They were going still, as they had always gone, and it was no longer the bite and the sup that drew them. They were going from the good lands as well as from the bad lands, from the lush Munster valleys and from the bare Atlantic coast. Emigration had become a habit.

"I'll bring you your tea in a minute, Brother."

"Time enough, child. Time enough."

He had all the time in the world.

He got up after lunch, levering his feet slowly from beneath the clothes, and sitting on the edge of the bed for a while like a swimmer dallying on the end of a springboard. It was strange how a few weeks in bed could make standing upright an achievement and walking an adventure. You grew tired of bed, but you were loath to leave it.

He put on shirt and trousers, and lathered himself for shaving. The face in the mirror hardly seemed worth the bother of shaving. It was gaunt, and wrinkled, and blotchy, and very, very old. It was so old that he laughed at it. He had never had much time to bother about his face, and now it took him by surprise. It wasn't anything to write home about, but it would do him for the rest of his time.

He felt better when he was washed and shaved. Then he wraped himself in the dressing gown that was not his or anybody else's but belonged to the

197 .

community and could be borrowed like a library book. He sat to rest himself for a few minutes, and then he went out to the corridor for a spell of sentry-go.

This exercised his limbs but brought no ease to the spirit. He was hemmed in by smooth aseptic walls that blunted his thoughts. After fifteen minutes of patrolling he went down to the chapel and said his prayers. They were dry, arid prayers, and he found it hard to keep his mind on them. After that he went back to his room and sat in the arm-chair by the window looking out on the city, on a world where people moved and worked and laughed and filled their lungs. He was a prisoner in a place where the days were long and the nights longer, where everything was timed and expected, where the schedule never varied. He was tired of it all.

He went back to bed after his tea, and when Sister Augustine came in later and asked him how he felt he answered her with grumbles. And she rounded on him. She told him that he was flying in God's face and not acknowledging His goodness. She reminded him that he would get down to Mass in the morning and said that he should count his blessings.

But there was no venom in her chiding nor depth in his grumbling. They understood one another.

On Christmas Eve morning he got down to the chapel under his own steam and knelt in the back seat between a gallstones and a hernia. He hobbled to the altar for Holy Communion, and he made a long thanksgiving. He felt happier than he had felt for many a day. He felt stronger too, but his strength drained from him as he climbed the stairs (Sister Augustine lectured him afterwards for not taking the lift), and after breakfast he was glad enough to sit by the window and look out at the city.

It was a long day. Paul was his only visitor. He left his parcels on the locker with the air of one explaining his presence, and then stood waiting. Paul never began a conversation. He was blessed with inarticulateness, and his tongue had never offended.

"Sit down, Paul. Sit down."

Paul sat as if he had a basket of eggs under him.

"I can't stay, Brother Bernard. You know how it is."

Bernard knew how it was. Christmas Eve in St. Michael's was a crowded and arduous vigil, full of bustle and flurry and happiness, with a great crush of last minute penitents, and preparations for the community Midnight Mass, and for breakfast and dinner the day after. It was the shortest day in the year, and it made him lonely to think of it.

"You'll have your hands full today, son."

"Indeed I will. I wish you were back."

"You don't wish it half as much as I do. They should have let me out for Christmas."

"It's God's will."

Paul was humble, and he had no load of learning, but he could put you in your box.

"You know, Paul, you should have been a novice master."

Paul looked shocked. He had as much chance of becoming Pope.

"You shouldn't say things like that, Brother Bernard. I must be off now. I wish you a happy and a holy Christmas."

199 .

For Paul, this was quite a long speech; and it was as near the lyric note as he ever got.

It was the longest Christmas Eve Bernard had ever known. But it was not lonely. He did a power of praying. He said his beads till he nodded over them, he read the Proper of the three Christmas Day Masses, and he prayed for his dead: for his father and mother, aunts and uncles; for Father Dan, and Sam Garnley, and the Flapper Flanagan; for Hughie, and Maurice Roarty, and his brothers in Christ. He prayed for them and to them.

He asked them to pray for a half-hearted religious, for one who didn't count his blessings, or pray hard enough; for an old man who grumbled when he should give thanks, and who wanted to pick and choose; who was only trotting behind Brother Paul and who had to remind himself constantly of first principles that the novice-master had dunned into him fifty years before; for the shadow of a religious who forgot that the Christ Child came to crowds and solitude, to hospital rooms and lighthouses and prisons and public houses, and that because of Him there could be no loneliness anywhere now or ever more.

18 .

He awoke early on Christmas morning. There was still a grey half-light in the rectangle of the window, but already the sky had a luminous quality, and even before his thoughts had sorted themselves from the confusion of sleep he knew the day it was and the reason for his exultation. It was always like that on Christmas Day and on Easter morn. The silence seemed like the echo of a great concourse of bells.

He was dressed and shaved before Michael knocked on his door, and he was first in the chapel. He felt young and happy, and there was a bite to his prayers. He heard his three Masses, and he took a long time to his thanksgiving. He had a lot to be thankful for.

Afterwards he walked up and down the corridor for a while. The whole mobile population was parading there. They were wishing each other a happy Christmas, and amazed to think that they were possibly going to have one. The gloom and resignation of the vigil had been replaced by the glory of the feast.

After a mighty breakfast he went over his Christmas presents. He had never had so many presents before. Lar Kerrigan from the market had sent him six cigars in torpedo cylinders; and the community had sent him a bottle of Beaujolais, and a hundred cigarettes, and a box of chocolates. The community, evidently, wanted him to have a good, hearty pagan Christmas as well as a holy one.

He went visiting then. He tapped at doors and sat on beds. He gave cigarettes to every hand that reached. He shared his chocolates, and gave two of his cigars to the bald man who had been operated on for gallstones. The place was full of visitors, and regulations had gone by the board. Two days before, the patients had been as lonely as convicts. Now they realized incredulously that they were a community and that they were going to have a happy Christmas.

Gallstones was in tremendous form. He wanted Bernard to have a glass of whiskey. Bernard didn't want any whiskey, but he went with Gallstones on a tour of the other rooms and they had doled out a good third of the bottle before Sister Augustine put an end to their gallivanting and whisked them back to their own quarters.

Bernard sat in his room then until Siobhan brought him his turkey and ham and plum pudding. He drank a glass of Beaujolais with his dinner, and he bribed Siobhan with a box of chocolates to bring a glass down to old Gallstones.

Afterwards, he smoked a cigar and drank another

glass of wine, which made him feel very benign, and very full, and a little sleepy. He had a succession of visitors from the monastery—Kilian and the Prior together, then Paul and Colman, and lastly Austin. But he didn't let them stay long. He knew the sacrifice they had made in coming, so he chased them as soon as he could and thought of the fun they were missing.

The monastery Christmas dinner was one of the highlights of the year. In St. Michael's, frugal living was the rule, but a feast was always a feast, and this was the biggest of them. There was red wine and white wine, and whiskey for those who wanted it. Even old Brother Joachim, who was pushing ninety, would have a drop of the crathur with his turkey, and smoke a cigar awkwardly, and say nothing at all until he was called on—as he was always called on—to start the concert with "The Banks of My Own Lovely Lee."

They all had their party pieces. The Prior fancied himself as a reciter, and he always gave them a gapped and imperfect rendering of "Shamus O'Brien." He lost his place several times as a rule, accepted promptings humbly, and came into the home stretch with a great burst of confidence.

> The soldiers ran this way,
> The sheriff ran that,
> And Father Malone lost his new Sunday hat.

Kilian sang a music hall song, with a most unmonastic chorus, in which the whole community joined—with the exception of old Brother Con, who disapproved of such worldliness:

> Down lovers' lane we'll wander,
> Sweetheart you and I,

Wait till the sun shines, Nellie,
By and by.

Bernard's songs were "O'Donnell Abu" and "Oft in the Stilly Night." He could have sung them in his sleep, and Kilian said that he sometimes did.

And with God's help, and a little assistance from the community with the high notes, he would sing them next Christmas Day. It was good to think of it. It had been touch and go, but his reprieve had come through.

He had never liked the end of December. It was the tail-end of the year, a dreary, dragging stretch of days, a sort of no man's land in time that belonged neither to the old year or the new. But the thought of what was to follow would help him to bear it. Before the days began to lengthen noticeably he would be back with his own, and the turn of the year would give a lift to his heart.

He would see the bitter days, and the snows of February, and the hard, black frosts. He would walk in the garden and time the rise of the sap in his apple trees, and know that the sap would be rising too in all the trees of Ireland from Cape Clear to the Swilly water. Life would stir in microscopic black buds close-wrapped against the cold, and little flecks of green would show in bark and branch as soon as the ice began to melt in the roadside ruts. Then the ploughmen would walk behind their horses and the brown earth that had been raked fine by the comb of the weather would fold upwards and break into crumbling billows; and the seagulls would come in leisurely squadrons and stand like giant hailstones against the mold.

The tractors would tug and rock across the fields on their serrated wheels, the teeth of the harrow would smash the clods, and the tiny seeds would swell and burst, would die and give birth, and there would be a rash of greenness everywhere. All life depended on this. It was the continuing rhythm of God's continuing creation. Thine the heavens and Thine the earth; the world and the fullness thereof Thou hast founded. It was the crisis of the year. If the miracle failed once, nothing that breathed or moved would live to see another spring.

But from now on his own husbandry would be rationed. He would be a ticket-of-leave man. He would be living on borrowed time, and the regulations would be strict for a while. Mr. Williamson would give his instructions, and Kilian and the Prior would see that they were carried out. He would be under double obedience.

But there were ways and means. He would get Paul to do the heavy digging, and he himself would do the trimmings. There could be no danger, surely, in planting shallots or dropping lettuce seed into a furrow that Paul had made. He could still spray his apple trees and do a little scuffling. There was a place for him yet. And at the worst he could walk about and keep his eyes open, watching for the first crocus and waiting for the daffodils. There were only a few daffodils in the monastery garden, but they were as sure a sign of the spring as great clumps in woodland parks, and one swallow could make a summer.

Siobhan brought him cold turkey and ham for his tea, and a slice of rich, iced cake in honor of the day that was in it.

"Ah, child, I couldn't face turkey twice in the same day," he said. "I'll just take a cup of tea."

But he ate most of the meat, and he finished the

cake down to the last crumb of icing. He lit a cigarette then, and he was just finishing it when Sister Augustine came in.

"There'll be a little concert in the library at seven o'clock," she said. "Maybe you would like to come to it?"

"A concert?"

"And a good one, too. We get some very good artists on Christmas Day. They do the rounds of the hospitals."

"Aye, I might go down. It might do me good. But what I would really need now is a week of fasting after all this feeding."

"Ah, well. Sure Christmas only comes once a year, and soon it will be as far away as ever."

"Aye, true enough. But I've had a long day. I'm thinking it might be no harm if I gave the concert a miss. I think I'll just sit here in the chair for a little while and then go to bed."

Sister Augustine nodded her head. "If you're feeling tired, that's the wise thing to do."

"I'm getting sense in my old age."

"Better late than never," she said.

"I've had a grand Christmas, thank God, and it would be foolish to overdo it. And I'm looking forward to getting home."

"You won't feel it till the new year."

"And after that, spring will come with a gallop. The worst of the winter is still ahead of us, no doubt, but it will be short and sharp. Once you begin to notice a stretch in the evenings it won't be long till the buds break. The thought of it keeps my heart up."

"I don't know whether you're a philosopher or a poet, Brother," she said.

"Just a foolish old man," he said. "I'm glad to be

206 .

alive, and I hope God will spare me for a little while."

He lay awake that night, thinking of the wakening earth. It was the way his thoughts were turning. He saw the dark-green crowns of potato plants pushing up along the drills, the wonder of the sprouting corn, the flowering of hawthorn and lilac and laburnum, the pattern and progress of growth. He saw gardens of rank kale with leaves that were green or purple as the light caught them, the silver tracks of snails on loose stone walls, the blackness of bog pools, and the glossy flanks of straining horses. He thought of harrow-time and seed sowing, of how the whins that seemed always in blossom would break into flame and run like fire along the flanks of the hills, and of how the fruit of the mountain ash would gather volleys of pillaging thrushes.

The corn would bleach and turn to gold and fall in swathes before the reaper, the tiny blueberries would ripen among the heather, the sloes would shine like grapes. The geese would scavenge in the stubble fields, the peats would be carted home, and then, before the main-crop potatoes were lifted, the swallows would muster.

He saw the dark Glen as clearly as if he had never left it. He listened to the sounds of it: the squirt and frothing of milk in shadowy byres, the nuzzling of calves' heads in zinc buckets, the creak of the half-door, the barking of dogs from across the Big Burn, the ring of scythe on whetstone, the rasping wakefulness of the corncrake.

The new year lay ahead, and he would time its ripening. It would be more magical than any that had gone before it, because it was an extension, a remand, an unlooked-for bonus. From now on

207 .

he would live to a formula, shelling peas in the kitchen, walking sedately beneath his apple trees, and putting no burden on his stiffening arteries. Death would come then, not clamorously, as it had come on Capel Street Bridge, but by a process of slow attrition. He would live on in St. Michael's, losing a little bulk and substance every year, drying out like a leaf at the foot of a tree, until in the end there would be nothing left to suffer and he would go out as effortlessly as a sigh.

All this was a comforting conviction, not a hope or a prayer. He made no demands, asked no boon. But for what time was left to him he would sit in the sun, and say his beads, and praise God in all that He had made, thinking of field and furrow, seed time and harvest, and the sound of the shingle at Bonn na dTonn. His end would be like his beginning.

There was danger there, as Austin had often told him, the danger that you might measure God by His handiwork and rate Him by His achievements and your own tiny grasp of them. But it was a tiny danger if you accepted all that was dogmatic and of faith, and you would have all eternity to get your sights right.

There was no reason, he thought, why he should not be home for New Year's Day. He would badger the sisters and doctors to let him go. They had no call to keep him any longer. Medicine could be carried about in bottles, and he could rest as well in the monastery as in a hospital bed—maybe better, for his mind would be at peace there.

Tomorrow would be St. Stephen's Day, and it would be too much to hope that Mr. Williamson would be stepping about so soon after the holiday,

208 .

but he would tackle him again at the first opportunity. The big man had given him a promise, and he would hold him to it. He would go home in spite of them. He had been here long enough.

He thought of New Year's Eve in the monastery, within a stone's throw of the quays and of Christchurch and St. Patrick's. You lay awake in spite of yourself, waiting for the great pagan clamor. It began with the screaming of sirens from ships and factories, baying to one another like wolves in a pack, and rising in their turn to a screaming crescendo. Then the bells joined in exultantly, rollicking and clattering in great tumbles of sound. In the end all pattern, all separateness was lost, and each component sound merged in one tuneless symphony that rose to a mighty climax and thinned almost imperceptibly as the brazen throats tired one by one and the sirens slithered down from the startingling heights and whimpered into silence.

You went to sleep then, thinking how this madness would strike New York in five hours' time, and spread across the continent to St. Paul and Minneapolis and then to Seattle and the Pacific. You went to sleep thinking of people: people in houses, people in streets, people in ships; people listening at high windows, or dancing in paper hats; people joining hands and clinging together for comfort; feeling a little lost and lonely and afraid, but looking hopefully to the future and putting their faith in the turn of a calendar leaf and wishing one another a bright and prosperous New Year. They were unknown and distant and anonymous, but they were all in God's list. You had links with them and duties towards them. You were part of a community that stretched through space and time.

209 .

When you prayed properly you prayed for the living and the dead; for every man Jack of them: without favor or ommission—and without ceasing.

In his present mood he could be magnanimous to all mankind. He was full of good food and good wine. But that was not the kind of magnanimity that God asked. He was a demanding God. He had given everything and He asked everything. A vague goodwill towards your fellow men was not enough. You had to wash their feet, and bind their sores, and embrace them when they stank, and welcome their jibes. You were to love until it hurt. You were to be like Francis in Assisi and like John in Granada. You were to seek God in the Flapper Flanagan and Sam Garnley and not in clouds and sunsets. It was easy to love humanity in general, but it was not easy to love the tramp on the doorstep.

You had to welcome suffering, not in a mood of virtuous resignation, but because it was what you deserved. And in this test, Bernard felt, he had failed badly. He had regarded his sufferings on the bridge and in the hospital bed as regrettable misadventures, and now he was bespeaking comfort for the rest of his days. Comfort was the dry rot of the soul. It made you purr and preen yourself. Suffering was cleansing and revealing. It drew you out of the shell of the self, like a winkle on a pin. It left you naked and alone. It scoured you with the salt of self-knowledge.

He still needed scouring, and maybe God would send it. Perhaps in His mercy He would deny him ease for the years that were left to him and send him pain in the measure of his weakness. If he sat in the sun, and planted shallots, and remembered the purple hills—if he did but this and then went out as effortlessly as a sigh he would go with one hand as long as the other.

It was time that he started to give. He knew where his heart was, and where his treasure was, and it was time to disburse. Field and flower could keep you from God as surely as yellow gold. He must strip himself and empty his coffers, tearing himself from sights and sounds, from the rattle of turf carts on mountain roads and the sharp ping of blackberries in tin pandies, from fuchsia and hawthorn and the early crocus, from the ebony-green of the opening buds and the milk of the apple blossom. He would have to sign over even his apple trees, to tear up the roots that were deeper than their roots in the brown clay. He would have to give and give until there was nothing left, and what he had to give was the green earth, to give it back to where it belonged. Thine the heavens and Thine the earth; the world and the fullness thereof Thou hast founded.

At last he had the link between Father Austin's theology and his own. Loving God's creation led you to love Him in His creation, and then you were only half-roads to the truth. This was spiritual childhood, and you had to grow out of it. God gave you the world to enjoy, but He wanted it back. He gave it to you as a sign, and waited then until you no longer needed a sign. You had to stretch out and up without the help of steppingstones. God was not just to be admired as a craftsman and architect. He was to be loved and adored for Himself. If you offered Him body and soul, will and intellect, it was a sorry contradiction to hold back sunsets and keep a lien on your four apple trees.

There was a gap in this reasoning, he felt, but he

211 .

could not puzzle it out. Austin would piece it together for him later on. Or perhaps it was that he had taken too much of the Beaujolais. He was not used to high living. Now the thing was to go to sleep. He had had a long day, and a tiring one, and he had a lot to be thankful for.

It would be good to get back to St. Michael's. He could pray there. He would have plenty of time for praying now.

He had a week to wait for the New Year, but he seemed to hear already the thin wail of a siren, and the happy jangling of bells—muted, as if the sound came sleepily across a summer valley. He felt very drowsy and very happy. The time would not be long passing. He would be going home very soon.

19.

Sister Magdalena had had a tiring day, for the spirit of Christmas seeps in even to hospitals. There had been streams of visitors all day long, and discipline had been eased in honor of the feast. And then, in the middle of it all, a teenage girl had been rushed in with peritonitis, and that had meant phoning inaccessible surgeons and urging St. Joseph to ferret one out and hurry him on. In hospital work there was no respite, no truce of God. You kept your fingers crossed and hoped for the best.

It was after eleven, and that was late for Magdalena. She should have been in bed an hour since. But things were doing nicely. The peritonitis case was in no immediate danger, and a special night nurse had come on duty at ten. It had been a trying day, but there would be a long lie-in in the morning, for on St. Stephen's Day the community Mass was at the unusually late hour of seven-thirty. Magdalena promised herself a nice long sleep, and she felt that she had earned it. She would wake and doze off again, and revel in the luxury of it. It was not often that she revelled in luxury.

Meanwhile, she had a few last-minute jobs to do. She had to visit the young fellow in number 38 —his wound had turned tricky and was not healing as quickly as she would have liked. She had to have a peep at the old Canon in 15 and Brother Bernard in 29. They were both off the danger list, but with heart cases you never knew. Besides, they were both old men—the Canon was doddering—and old men were like children. They went to sleep happily when they had been tucked in; they felt more secure when they knew that there was someone on guard.

Old patients were apt to be querulous and dependent and in need of comforting. She liked them that way. The best people, she often thought, became a little crotchety with the years. They became like little children. They were not worldy-wise, or philosophical, or even patient.

The old Canon was a little grumpy when she spoke to him. But she knew that he was pleased. Now he would turn over and go to sleep. Bernard was the last on her list. His room was in darkness, so she crept in and turned on the little lamp. Then she knelt down and said an Act of Contrition in his ear, keeping a finger pressed on the alarm bell. It would flash in the little office where Nurse Kelleher was yawning, and in the front office where Michael was watching the switchboard.

But Magdalena's place was at the bedside. She kept praying and praying.

Father Denbigh had a long, tiring day, a frustrating day. He had said seven o'clock Mass, and had been Deacon at the midday High Mass, and after that he had been "on calls," sitting beside a telephone that never rang, watching like a sentry, keeping guard against the old old enemy. He was spancelled and tethered. Had he been free, he could have had his Christmas dinner with his sisters in Sandycove, or with a married brother in Templeogue, but now his tether did not stretch as far as that, and all it permitted him was dinner in the Canon's, which was only a furlong away.

At the best of times, dinner in the Canon's was not very exciting. The old man gave a good meal, and prided himself on his knowledge of wines, but he was pompous in a courtly sort of way, and he had an exaggerated idea of the gulf that separated curates from parish priests. The company, too, was a little grim: an ancient sister who was almost completely deaf, and a wizened solicitor cousin who spoke as if he were on oath.

Father Denbigh had to leave at five o'clock, when the room was filling with cigar smoke and tedious reminiscence, for he was still on duty. He went back to his own house and relieved Mary, his housekeeper, who had manned the listening post during his absence, and who left immediately to spend the evening with her niece in Ballybough. He was on his own then.

He sat in an armchair, smoking interminably, listening to the wireless and dozing over a crossword. It would have been a relief to hear the telephone and answer an urgent summons, but there wasn't a cheep out of it all evening. It was Christmas Day, and no one died on Christmas Day if he could help it.

At eight o'clock, he made tea and drank it in the kitchen. Then he went back to the room, poured himself a glass of sherry that he didn't want, and read a detective story until he tired of it. It was a long, long evening.

Mary came back at half-past ten.

"Maybe you would like to go out for a while, Father?"

"I think I will, Mary. I might run down to O'Reilly's for an hour or so. If any calls come you could ring me up there. That is, if you don't mind sitting up."

Mary didn't mind. She had been a priest's house-keeper for thirty years, and she was used to her own company. She lived to rule, like a confined religious. She made meals, and said her prayers, and rose betimes.

There was a game of poker in O'Reilly's, and a great buzz of talk. Father Denbigh squeezed in at the table, and Mrs. O'Reilly brought him tea and cold plum pudding, in spite of his refusals. "You couldn't come to the house on Christmas Day without tasting the plum pudding."

Father Denbigh played poker badly but with enjoyment. He interrupted his own stories to ask who had opened the pot, and he sometimes played to Jokers which had been current in the last hand but one.

He had just said "I'll see your shilling and raise you a shilling" when the telephone rang, and he was putting down his straight to be beaten by a full house when Mrs. O'Reilly came in and said "It's for you, Father." Twelve minutes later he was giving Brother Bernard his last anointing.

Sister Magdalena was there, and Sister Augustine, and Nurse Kelleher, and Dr. Kerrigan, but their pooled strength was as nothing. There was a flicker in the poor pulse and an occasional flutter of the eyelids, but Bernard was going. No one mattered now but Father Denbigh, who had had a long day and a miserable evening, and who had lacked the gumption to notice that Sam O'Reilly never set down his pipe unless he had the whale of a hand.

Father Denbigh was in charge now, and his bailiwick reached to the stars. He was at the Canon's beck and call, but he could summon the saints, and call on great Michael who stood before the Throne, and give the demons the back of his hand. He could beg the Lord—he could almost order Him, since he spoke in His name—to deliver His servant Bernard as He had delivered Daniel and Susanna and David and Saul. Nothing evil could stand against him. He was the King's man. The angels were round his head and the heavens stopped to listen.

It was all over, and the room was very quiet. Father Denbigh was back to size now. He was a poor poker player, and a bit of a gabbler, and he was losing his hair. He was the Canon's man.

He rolled his stole round his finger, ceding his glory.

"He went quietly in the end."

"Like a child," said Sister Augustine.

"Did he suffer much?"

"A little in the beginning," said Magdalena, "but not much. He was unconscious when I came in to him—or very near it."

"Did he speak at all?" asked Father Denbigh.

Magdalena shook her head. "I spoke to him, but he didn't answer me."

Then she went on. "When I was saying the Act of Contrition he was trying to say something, but I couldn't catch much of it, and what I did catch didn't make sense. Something about apple trees and green corn. He must have been raving, the poor man. But God was good to him, and he had a lovely death."

Sister Augustine spoke then, but very quietly, as if she was speaking to herself; Sister Augustine, who had warm brown eyes and had been reared in the orchard country of Kilkenny.

"He babbled of green fields," she said.

"What's that?" said Magdalena sharply.

"Nothing at all," said Augustine. "Nothing at all. I was just thinking."